Love at First Sight

CHERYL BARTON

Published by: Cheryl Barton Publishing, LLC

Cheryl Barton Publishing, LLC
P.O. Box 962
Reisterstown, Maryland 21136
www.crbarton.com

Ordering Information:
Quantity sales. Special discounts are available on quantity purchases by corporations, associations, and others. For details, contact the publisher at the address above.

Orders by U.S. trade bookstores and wholesalers.
Please contact prez@crbarton.com

ISBN: 1948950006
ISBN-13: 978-1-948950-00-8

Other books by Cheryl Barton

Bachelor Series

Bachelor Not for Sale
A Designed Affair
A Perfect Combination
Love at Last
Twelve Bachelors for Sale – Coming 2018

Amorous Occupations Series

The Artist
The Bookkeeper
The Chef
The Dancer
The Electrician

A Lovers' Heart

Heartthrob
Heartbeat – Coming 2018

Second Chances Series

Snowbound
Cupid's Arrow
One Wish

Stand Alone Romance

Holly for Christmas
Un-Break My Heart
Bossy
Love on Top
My First Love
Black Love

For the lover in you!

Chapter 1

Kimara Banks felt a bone-chilling cool breeze in the air as she sat in her office trying to concentrate on the stack of files that sat in front of her, knowing she needed to give them her full attention in order to get caught up on work that had been piling up for days. The only thing she found herself accomplishing was a focused and very detailed inspection of the pale white wall in front of her with the large African-Safari picture that took up too much of the wall space. The animal lover in her wouldn't allow her to take it down and find something small. The picture had been there for over a year, but until today, she hadn't realized how much space it really took up.

For some reason, her day seemed off and she found herself noticing things that had, in the past, fit naturally into her large, expansive office on the eighth floor of the downtown Houston office park where she worked as a marketing consultant. Her mind was all over the place and as hard as she tried, she couldn't seem to reign it in to achieve greater focus on the tasks at hand.

Her plans for a relaxed day at work playing catch up

seemed to be invaded by an uncomfortable feeling, one she couldn't seem to shake. Kimara shivered when that cook breeze engulfed her again. She wouldn't be bothered if it wasn't for the fact that the chill had nothing to do with the air streaming through the vents along the base of the floor, even though it was cool because of the hotness of the summer June day. The cold chill was felt along her spine and not on the surface of her skin. The scratchy feeling that made her want to rub her back against the high-back brown leather chair wasn't going away, but instead, continued to nudge at her like a warning. A warning of what, she thought?

Distracted, Kimara practically leaped out of her chair the moment her office phone rang, startling her by the sudden intrusion. She reached for it and then hesitated as that uncomfortable feeling smacked her across the face like an ice-cold rag. Remembering to breathe, she hit the speaker phone button after seeing her sister Casey's number appear on the lit up blue screen. She was about to speak with her usual cheerful greeting when she was interrupted.

"Kim, are you watching the news?" Casey asked before she had the chance to get a word out.

Kimara sat straight up in her chair, as concern wavered around her by the seriousness of her sister's voice. Without being able to see Casey's face, something in her town let her know that Casey wasn't smiling happily and about to initiate one of their daily girl chats. Something was wrong, she thought, as she waited to hear Casey's next words. There was something in the way she spoke that put her on high alert.

She finally found her voice.

"The news? Why would I be watching the news while in the office. What's happening on the news?" she asked, not sure she really wanted to know.

She loved hearing from Casey, but never has she called without first saying hello.

"What are you doing right now?" Casey asked seriously.

Kimara didn't sense even a hint of the jovial, sisterly greeting Casey often used. This time she heard a strange, eeriness to the tone of her voice. It rang loudly through the phone like an annoying bull horn. Her heart began to beat faster as thought after thought raced through her mind of a million scenarios of bad situations going on. Was she sick? Did something happen to their mother? What was it? Kimara braced herself for the impact of whatever Casey had to say.

No longer comfortable with sitting still, she stood up and walked around to the front of her desk, leaning back against it, crossing her legs at the ankles with feet covered in her favorite grey five-inch stilettos that were a perfect match to the color of her two-piece suit. Bracing her hands on either side of her on the desk, she exhaled to calm her nerves and hoped that the inkling that there was something major happening would dissipate.

"What is it Casey? You know I get nervous when you start beating around the bush and not giving things to me straight, so spill it," she warned.

Before Casey had a chance to respond, Kimara looked to her right through the large glass pane, the only one that had the blinds open that gave her a clear view of the outer office space. Stirring her nerves even more, she noticed that some of the staff were running toward the conference room on their floor, the only room that had a television besides her office and the offices of the company executives. She hardly ever turned hers on which she knew could lead to a day full of distractions. There was a pause and she knew Casey was struggling to tell her something. It was time for her to turn on the television that sat on the stand between the two bay windows that overlooked the downtown Houston sky. She looked around for the remote.

"Have you talked to Ellis? I know you dropped him off earlier this morning to catch the train. Has he checked in with you yet? I know it's only been a few hours," Casey said.

Kimara paused. Casey asked about her husband, the love of her life, Ellis. Kimara was now on the verge of sheer panic.

"You're calling about Ellis? Why? What does this conversation have to do with Ellis?" she asked, now openly panicking.

Now worried beyond belief, she frantically looked around for the remote, jerking her head left, then right before stooping to look under her desk. She would have called out to her assistant who sat right outside of her office, but like everyone else, she had caught a glimpse of her jetting to the conference room. Whatever was going on had to be big, she thought.

"Kim, I'm on my way to your office. I'm a few blocks away and I'll be there in a few minutes," Casey said and Kimara could almost swear she sounded as if she were on the brink of tears. Seeing the remote sitting in the corner of the leather sofa, she grabbed it, turned toward the television and clicked it on. Not knowing what she was looking for, she feverishly searched through the channels before landing on a news channel with the words scrolling across the screen that said, 'Breaking News'.

In an instant, her heart seemed to stop beating when she read the message that scrolled across the bottom of the screen with more words as images of large plumes of smoke filled the screen and the lights of emergency vehicles flashed everywhere. She also saw a helicopter flying high above what appeared to be a horrible accident.

"A train crash!" she screamed out loud and then covered her mouth as if she'd uttered something she should not have.

"Kimmy, hold it together. I'm almost there. I didn't mean to upset you and I'm sure Ellis is fine and wasn't on that particular train. Either way, I'll be at your office in a few minutes. Why don't you try and call Ellis and I'll call him, too? I'm sure one of us will reach him and he'll be fine, okay?" Casey encouraged.

Kimara didn't hear anything she said. As her heart raced a million miles a minute, she disconnected the call with Casey and dialed Ellis' cell phone. After several rings, the phone went into his voicemail. Ellis Banks, the love of her life for the past four years wasn't answering.

With a shaky voice on the brink of crying she said, "Ellis, baby, it's me. Call me as soon as you get this message. I'm in the office, so either phone will be fine. Call me," she said and tried not to sound like she was panicking.

Hanging up without waiting for him to respond to her message, she quickly dialed him again and again and again and each time, she received the same result – Ellis didn't answer.

Kimara didn't know what to do. She felt like she couldn't breathe as she continued dialing Ellis' phone over and over, praying that one of the times, he would answer, but he didn't. Trying to remain calm, she turned up the volume on the television and tried to understand what the announcer was saying. She listened as the woman on the screen noted the train departure number, so that any family that had a loved one on the train could contact a number on the screen for more information. While the room around her seemed to spin and she began to feel dizzy, Kimara reached for her purse to find the note where she had scribbled the train information Ellis had quoted to her once he had his arrangements for travel.

Finding everything inside of her designer bag except the kitchen sink, she turned it upside down and looked for the bright pink post-it note with the information on it.

Before finding the small scrap of paper, tears began to form in her eyes, wondering if her day was about to turn into a nightmare. Opening up the folded piece of paper, she glanced at what she'd written and looked up at the television screen to see that what was on her piece of paper, matched what the announcer gave as the train that was involved in the accident.

Staring in wonderment at the screen and not knowing what to do, she held her breath as images of Ellis mangled in the wreckage she saw fed her fear and then her world crashed around her. Her body shook as her legs began to give way. She could feel her body about to collapse to the floor when she felt herself being held up by comforting arms.

"I got you, sis," Casey said, "I got you. Why don't you have a seat and I'll keep trying Ellis' phone."

Kimara did sit down and stared at the wall unable to think or feel as numbness overcame her.

"Ellis was on that train," she stuttered out, trying to hold back her tears.

"What? How do you know that?" Casey replied as she pulled out her cellphone and began dialing her brother-in-law's number, hoping upon everything that he would answer. She turned and looked to where Kimara was pointing at a small pink piece of paper that was lying on the floor. Casey picked it up, saw what was written on it and then looked up at the television screen and sure enough, the information matched exactly. Now, she shared what she knew her sister was feeling, but she had to keep a strong façade to remain hopeful for them both.

"That's his train engulfed in all that smoke, in all that wreckage," Kimara said in a way that even shocked her. Her words held no emotion just as she wasn't feeling any. She was afraid to move or do anything when what she needed most was to hear Ellis' voice.

"There's a number on the screen that they're saying family can call to get the latest on the crash," Casey said.

Kimara didn't care about a number to call. She needed to get to Ellis and see for herself that he was okay. Finding the little bit of strength she could muster up, she stood, walked over to her office chair and grabbed her suit jacket. In the pile of items that had been in her purse that were now scattered across her desk, she spotted her wallet and car keys, picked them up along with her cell phone and tried to focus on what she needed to do next. Holding her composure in check and trying to be positive, she straightened her skirt, turned her thoughts to seeing Ellis alive and well and headed for her office door.

"I'm not dialing any number. I'm going to head to the train station where it looks like others are already gathering according to the news. Even though the crash site is over an hour away, I doubt if I can get close to that, but being at the train station here is something. I'm sure other families are gathering there and if any news is going to be given out, I'm sure the families will get that first-hand there. Let's go," she said without looking back.

With powerful, hurried strides, Kimara made her way toward the elevator, past the conference room and went to find her husband. Casey spoke behind her as they waited for the elevator to reach their floor.

"I'm sure Ellis is fine, sis."

"I don't know, Casey. If he were okay, he knows I would have heard about the accident by now and would be worried. He would have done everything in his power to try and call me and so far, I haven't heard anything which worries me. I have to get there."

Casey felt her sister's pain and knew that no more words were going to be exchanged for now. No one in the world was closer to her than her sister and when she was hurt and worried, Casey knew they shared those emotions. She would be whatever her sister needed her to be and it didn't matter how bad the situation got. Casey held her head up, reached for Kimara's hand as the elevator door opened and stepped inside with her. She looked at Kimara.

"I'm with you," she said as the elevator doors closed.

**

Brody Grey whizzed in and out of traffic, making his way to his office for a day filled with one meeting after another. His first appointment was due to arrive in about fifteen minutes and he was over thirty minutes away.

"Call Maggie," he said to the car's hands-free phone system. Maggie, his executive assistant would look after his client until he arrived. She picked up immediately.

"Maggie, I'm on my way into the office, but I'm going to be

about fifteen minutes late for my first appointment this afternoon. I had to drop Peyton off at the train station this morning for a visit with her extended family for a few days while I wrap things up with that deal. If Ainsley Harrison gets there before I do, get him some coffee and order some pastries from across the street. I'm on my way and should be there shortly. I had to go back to my house to wait for a delivery that Peyton didn't tell me about until the last minute, so stall him if you need to. Don't let him leave. This is a big deal for us," he said.

Ainsley Harrison was bringing a major project to the bank for financing, one of the biggest deals of his career since he started working at the bank as one of it's vice presidents, one of the youngest around at age thirty.

"I've got it covered, Brody. Don't worry and don't drive like a crazy person to get here. I'm good at padding the extra time," Maggie said.

"You are a lifesaver, that's for sure."

"Now that we both know that, slow your car down to a respectable speed, turn on some music and I've got everything here under control until you get here for your meeting. I'll explain the situation and besides, Mr. Harrison has three children of his own and I'm sure he'll understand you making sure your wife, who is six months pregnant with your first child, was able to get to the train safely. Now, slow down," she said before disconnecting the call.

Brody laughed at Maggie's parting words. Only she would know that he was speeding through traffic. The business meeting was important and he hated being late, but more important to him than that meeting was Peyton and their baby girl who would be joining them in a few short months.

Time seemed to fly by the moment Peyton found out she was pregnant. As soon as they knew the baby was a girl, she had begun began filling the nursery he'd finally finished painting a month ago. The delivery he had to rush back home for was the new bedroom furniture she'd ordered. Their lives had become consumed with preparing for their daughter, the first of many children they wanted to have. The fact that it was a little girl excited him even more. He knew that most men wanted boys and so did he, but he was extra excited about their first being a little girl. He was looking forward to spoiling her and celebrating when her first word turned out to be 'Dada'. He and Peyton had a bet about whose name their daughter would say first.

His life was Peyton and their growing family. From the day they'd met and then eventually got married, his life had been next to perfect. Peyton, who worked as a nurse, was looking forward to taking an entire year off from work to raise and bond with their daughter. Wanting to make sure she could do that, he had been working extra hard at his job at the largest bank in Houston, Texas as the vice president of financial services specializing in corporate finance. His mother and twin sister took turns teasing him about how tight Peyton had him wrapped around her finger, but he knew he wouldn't change a thing. Whatever Peyton wanted, he would do whatever he could to make it happen and if she wanted an entire year to focus on their daughter, he would make sure they wanted or needed for nothing.

Now, taking his time getting to the office, Brody turned on the car radio just as a somber voice explained that there had been a train accident and it was a bad one. There were many passengers who were injured and that there were several fatalities, but no information was available on the number yet. Brody slammed on his brakes, causing the car behind him to honk annoyingly at him. He waited for more information and then dread seeped into every pore. As the announcer gave information about the train that was impacted, his life flashed before his eyes.

"Peyton!" he screamed. He had dropped his love off at the train station and he knew from the departure information the announcer gave that Peyton had been on that train. Without thinking twice, he turned his car around and headed in the direction of the train station never giving his meeting another thought.

Chapter 2
Five Years Later

Kimara was enjoying paradise on her first day of vacation on one of the most beautiful islands in the world, the island of Turks and Caicos. It's a place she had dreamed of going to for years, but never made the sacrifice of her time. If she had known that her life would be where it is now, without the love of her life at her side every day, she would have taken this trip and many others long before now, but to her, it's better to go late than to not go at all. Ellis would be proud of her taking this step, she thought.

For a brief second, Kimara felt sorrowful as memories flooded her mind the turn her life had taken and wished it had more meaning than she felt it had lately, especially when she thought of her beloved Ellis, the man who brought love into her life like she'd never experienced before. She wanted him with her, needed him with her, but knowing that it wasn't meant to be, she had to press on and make life work in this new circumstance. Thankfully, that included her trek to a magnificent island where she hoped to get a lot of rest, work hard to move on from the past and finally take the leap into a new self-imposed freedom from the life she had planned to live while walking into the destiny of a life that was still worth living, despite tragedy.

Kimara knew that as long as she kept waking up every day, this day, one she prayed would one day not bring her sadness, would come around again in another three hundred and sixty-five days, sixty-six days during leap year. For all of the people who said the day would get easier as years went by, had lied. For her it didn't seem to get easier as memories poured in daily and on this day, they tripled in their impact and on her ability to get through the day being able to focus on anything, but the day. The only thing different about this day, this year was the location in which she was spending it. She had to fight the sadness, the loneliness and the despair that followed her day in and day out and enjoy her time away from Houston, Texas even if it were only for a few days.

Walking across the brightly lit pathway to her villa after enjoying the best omelet and fresh fruit breakfast that she'd ever had, Kimara looked up at the sky where the sun was shining so bright, she squinted even though she was wearing dark sunglasses.

The day was extremely hot at ninety-five degrees, but wasn't humid, making it a little more enjoyable. The island was lovely and thanks to her mother and sister, she was staying at the most exquisite villa in Grace Bay. Her personal bungalow had one large bedroom with windows on three of the four walls and each overlooked the beautiful blue ocean water. The sitting area in the main room was her favorite place even though she'd only been on the island for one day. There was a chaise lounge where she sat for hours doing absolutely nothing and with as inviting as the chair looked and felt the moment she sat on it, she didn't want to do anything. She loved that the villa didn't have a television but was filled with a lot of books which was something she requested when she filled out the questionnaire asking about her needs prior to her arrival. She was happy to see that they were able to accommodate a stack of books by some of her favorite authors.

Her second favorite feature was the large bathroom that included a large claw-foot bathtub that sat in the middle of the room. Tonight, she was planning on lighting candles to enjoy some quiet time before deciding on whether to attend the night's festivities that were planned by the resort staff. Tonight, they were planning a movie night on the beach. Her first thought was she knew they were planning a different event each night and she still had four additional nights on the island before she had to return to her life. For tonight, she would skip the gathering and enjoy some alone time, but as she promised her sister, she would venture out for the rest of her stay.

Kimara could hear the chime of her cell phone and rushed to answer it. She already knew it was going to be either her mother or her sister calling to be sure she was having a good time, enjoying the blue waters on the beach, the incredible food and hopefully interacting with others who were on the island. She had to admit, the food was absolutely delicious, but she would have to lie about getting in the water and interacting with people. So far, she hadn't done those, but she knew it was best not to worry her family unnecessarily. She knew they were worried that she would wallow the entire time, but she honestly felt like she was over feeling sorry for herself. She had mourned and now it was time for her to find the bright side of life again.

Ellis dying in that train accident five years ago kickstarted a new path for her and now that path needed to be one of happiness and not sadness. Everyone suffered loss at one time or another, but for her, losing a mate wasn't just suffering a loss, it was like losing a part of her own body, her very own soul. She would honor Ellis by making the best of her trip and her life because she knew he would expect and want her to.

"I'm fine," Kimara said the moment she answered the phone without even checking to see who it was.

"Kim! I've been calling you for the past hour," her mother said.

Kimara walked across the soft, plush, velvety sky-blue carpet toward the bedroom where she laid across the soft down comforter while her mother rambled on. She knew it would be a lengthy conversation since she had not spoken to anyone in her family since the day before when she arrived on the island.

"Mom, I told you and Casey to stop worrying about me. I'm doing fine and I'm already enjoying myself. This villa is wonderful. I spent the morning exploring after arriving late yesterday and I'll do the same later tonight."

"You know I worry about you."

"I know mom. Where is Casey? I know she's lurking somewhere close by," she laughed.

"Well, it's good to hear you laugh," Casey said joining the conversation, most likely after picking up one of the other phone extensions in her mother's house.

"I knew you weren't too far away," Kimara said.

"How are the men? Any really sexy ones you want to bring

back to the states for your sister? You know how I like them!" Casey said.

"Uh, mom is on the phone – you know that, right?" Kimara asked.

"Yes, I am on here and can you both promise to keep it clean just for me? Casey you have a man!" their mother added.

Casey and Kimara broke out in laughter.

"We promise," they said together.

"I'm going to let you girls talk. I'm glad you're enjoying your time on vacation. I think it's exactly what you need. I want to hear all about it when you get home in a few days and I promise to keep your sister from bugging you every day. Have fun and I love you."

"I love you too, mom and as hard as you'll try to keep Casey from bugging me every day, she's going to try just as hard to counter that, so don't waste your time. Let her call and I'll decide if I'm going to answer or not," she joked.

"Hello, I am still on the phone!" Casey shouted.

"How could I forget," Kimara laughed.

"I'm not going to keep you. I heard momma say she was going to call you and I wanted to know how you were doing. Sounds like you're not just sitting around wallowing like you do when you're here at home and that's good to know. Have enough fun for me and go ahead and get you a little something from an islander, someone you'll never have to see again, but who can rock your world. Remember, it's just like riding a horse," Casey quipped.

"I know what it's like, sis," Kimara said and shook her head in disbelief even though Casey couldn't see her.

"Well, I wasn't sure since it's been such a long time. I was sure you forgot how that goes."

Kimara tried to stifle a laugh, but failed.

"Jokes, I see. We can't all be married to an incredible guy like your husband, Mike, who according to you, stirs up your amorous appetite for him on the regular."

"Yeah, well I expect you to be in that same kind of happy place again. Life and love didn't end for you five years ago. Your new mister right is waiting for you to be open to the possibilities of love again. I want that for you, Kimmy. You deserve to be happy like that again," Casey said.

"I know and when the time is right, I will be. I'm not saying it's not now or it may be in another five years. I'm not completely closing myself off to the idea that I will have love again. I do believe I'm ready for it."

"Then, in that case, I know for a fact it will happen. I'm happy to hear you're ready. You have had me worrying for a while now. What did you decide to do about the house? Are you still looking for that house with farm land for all those animals you want to raise? I've never heard of anything so crazy in my life. How does a city girl decide she wants a farm with animals? Besides, you moved into the condo, but you haven't sold the house yet."

"Don't knock what I love. I haven't decided on anything yet. I'm probably going to sell it when I return. The couple who has been renting it all these years has been asking the management company about purchasing it. It's that last big thing of my life with Ellis that I still have. It's time to let it go. I may just buy my farm," Kimara said.

She had struggled for years to sell the house that she and Ellis had bought together. It was time.

"Well, you certainly have the money to make your dreams

come true. Have you even touched any of the settlement money?" Casey asked.

Kimara along with all of the other families had received large financial settlements as a result of losing loved ones in the train accident and though most may have had immediate plans, she didn't and her money had been building interest for the past five years while she decided on her next step. For now, she was happy doing consulting work and spending time with family and friends back home.

"No, I haven't. I don't want to do anything frivolous and I always had plans to one day have a family and introduce my children to horses, cows, goats and chickens. My life may have changed, but I still want that."

"I have no doubt you will. I hope you still have plans of that big family you always wanted. You and Ellis didn't get there, but you still can. I am looking forward to being an auntie."

Kimara forced a smile, not for anyone to see, but to make herself feel good about the prospect of one day having her own children. At thirty-two, there as still a lot of time to have kids.

"One day, Casey. Perhaps one day. I'm hanging up now and I'll see you in a few days. Try not to call every second of every day so that I won't have to purposely ignore my only sister. I love you!" Kimara exclaimed.

"I love you, too and I'll love you even more if you bring back some pictures of island hunks."

"Girl, stop acting like Mike doesn't star in every one of your wild and crazy dreams. You know you don't want anyone, but him."

"You're right, but I like to make you smile and me talking

about hunky men seems to do the trick. Go ahead and find you one so that I can live vicariously through you."

"I'll try my best. I will promise you that I will have the time of my life while I'm here," she said.

"That's all I'm asking for," Casey replied.

"Goodbye sis!" Kinara hollered and hung up.

Looking around, she decided to start more adventures the next day. For the rest of this day, she would enjoy her villa and the large veranda with beautiful white rattan furniture that was made for enjoying the warm weather. She smiled knowing this was the vacation she needed in her life.

Chapter 3

"Brody Grey, if you miss your flight, I'm never speaking to you again. You made a promise to me that you would take this vacation and get away from the office for a few days. Yet, I walk into the office today and who do I see, but my boss in his Brooks Brothers suit on the phone handling a multi-million-dollar investment account. Why aren't you on your way to the airport and dressed in some comfortable jeans or a sweat suit or anything other than a suit?"

Brody exhaled and hung his head low. He had been caught by his assistant Maggie and he knew there would be hell to pay. What he thought would be a quick stop in the office to handle an outstanding issue with one of his clients turned into a two-hour conference call, but at least he was able to get the situation under control and everyone was still financially stable including his own financial state.

He took great pride in giving his clients one-on-one service whether it was a multi-million-dollar corporation who requested his services or the retiree who wanted to talk with him directly to get confirmation that the money he'd worked his entire life for was safe and still making him more money. He may specialize in corporate accounts, but he would never walk away from helping someone with mere dollars in their account, too. He held his head in shame, knowing he needed to get to the airport, but time got away from him. He knew he should not be conducting business on the first day of his vacation.

"Maggie, I promise you I still have time to get to the airport. My bags are in the back of my car and I brought a change of clothes with me to the office. It will take me a few minutes to go downstairs to the gym, change and jump in my car. I'll be at the airport in no time at all," he proclaimed, hoping to pacify her for a few more minutes.

Maggie smirked at him with that motherly warning he had grown accustomed to.

"No more work today!" she demanded.

"You know, if I wanted to be reprimanded, I'd call my mother. She has enough of that for all of her children, especially me," he said.

"Yeah, well, she has a reason to have a little extra for you. It's because you deserve to be reprimanded and often. You work too hard, too often and though your dedication to our customers is exemplary, you need the downtime. Hand me the headset," Maggie said and stretched her arm out to him.

Brody wasn't sure she was serious until he noticed there wasn't even a hint of a smile on her face. He stepped back out of her reach and went around behind his desk to grab a folder, trying his best to avoid eye contact.

"Okay, I have one last call and it will be a quick one and then I'm out of here, I promise," he pleaded.

"Brody Grey, I have never said this before, but desperate times call for desperate measures. I'm going to back out of this office, pick up my phone and call your mother. I think she'd be interested in hearing that her son, who is supposed to be on his way to the beautiful island of Turks and Caicos, is in the office, in business attire and negotiating business deals. She wouldn't be happy to hear that. Don't make me do it, Brody, now hand over the headset, grab your clothes, get changed and get out of here. This place can operate without you for a week."

"Wait, I'm only going to the island for five days," he said.

"Correct, but you're off for an entire week and that means seven days. I don't expect to see you come back in here before those seven days are up. I'm hoping you'll return so relaxed that you'll take a few more days off. You need this even if you don't realize it," she said.

Brody knew he was fighting a losing battle.

"I know and you're right."

"You haven't taken time off to just relax in a long time and you could use some downtime. You deserve this and I know it's June and what that means to you," she said and then wished she could take the words back. The impact of saying the month stopped Brody in his tracks and for that, she was sorrier than she could ever express to him.

Maggie started to say more and thought it best to be quiet and walk away. She didn't mean to bring up the month since everyone already walked on pins and needles this time of year whenever he was around.

"Don't walk away, Maggie. It's okay and trust me, I know you didn't mean any harm, though I can see on your face that you wish you could take back what you said. It's okay, really it is."

Brody exhaled and removed the headset from his head

and handed it to her. He was so wrapped up in work that for a few hours, the fact that it was June and the anniversary of Peyton's death had eluded him and for that he was happy. Now hearing it, all of the memories of Peyton came crashing down on him and the weight of the month crashed down as well. He missed Peyton and even more so, when June came around.

Maggie held her head down in shame at how careless and insensitive she was to what she knew was always a rough time for him.

"I'm sorry," she said softly, taking the headset from his hands and grasping it tightly in hers.

Brody was like a son to her since he was the same age as her own son. As a mother, she knew that he was in turmoil every year about this time. She should have known better than to bring up the obvious. The reason for him taking the vacation was so that he would get away from what June reminded him of and have some fun. She knew that he used work to mask his sorrow and for the first time in years, he was finally taking the advice of family and friends and taking the trip his friends had given him as a gift two years ago.

"Don't be. I know you didn't mean any harm and I know it's June. It brings sorrow, but it's also getting close to Journee's birthday and for that I'm excited. She'll be five in a month."

Exactly one month after the train crash, Journee had been born on the same day that Peyton had died. He didn't have a lot of time to grieve because he needed to be about life to take care of a newborn. Journee Peyton Grey was his happy ball of fire and everything about her said she was Peyton's daughter.

"She's getting so big. I hope you're planning a party," Maggie said, hoping to take the conversation into a happier direction.

"I am. My mother and sister are already making plans for a Disney themed tea party and in August, I'm taking her to Disney Land in California before she heads to school," he boasted.

"Oh, that'll be fun. Two vacations for you in one year, huh? I'm shocked and excited at the same time. I'm glad there are things that make you happy."

"So am I. Peyton would want me moving on and not dwelling on the sadness of this month."

"I know, but still, I shouldn't have thrown it in like that."

"It's okay. You're right that I need to get going. My flight leaves in two hours and I need to get moving."

Brody straightened up the disarray that was the top of his black marble-topped redwood desk. Now, he actually did feel back about stopping in the office when he should have steered his car in the direction of the airport. Not looking back, he grabbed what he needed and walked out. He had a five-hour flight to catch and though a little hesitant, he knew it was needed. The time away would be good and hopefully he could do more than reminisce about what could have been and learned more to enjoy the life he has now.

"Have a safe flight and have some fun. You're long overdue."

Brody was about to respond when his cell phone rang.

"I'm sure this is my sister telling me the exact same thing that you just said. I'll see you when I get back," he said, waving and turning toward the elevator.

"Hey sis!" he said answering.

"Are you at the airport?"

Brody cringed knowing if he lied she would know and if he told the truth, he would be in for a scolding.

"Brynne, I'm on my way there. You didn't need to check up on me. I'm not going to change my mind and not go," he said.

"Brody, don't you dare back out and you better not be at that office. That place can stand to be without you being there for a few days."

"I know and I only stopped by for a few minutes. I have two hours and my office isn't far from the airport."

"As your twin, I know you're lying to me and you've been there for more than a few minutes, but I'm going to let that lie slide. If you don't go on this trip, I'm never speaking to you again!" she declared.

Brody laughed. Everyone was threatening to not speak to him if he didn't make his flight. Brynne, of course, always brought her own level of drama to every conversation.

They were twins born a few minutes apart. Those few minutes made her the older sibling and she never let him forget it.

"Liar. If I committed a crime or needed to hide a body, you'd be there with me, helping me plan it out without asking any questions. I can always count on you and you wouldn't know what to do with yourself if you didn't talk to me every day or try to twin me into revealing all of my secrets. I am not going to miss my flight and I'm going to have so much fun, you won't recognize the well relaxed brother I will be when I return. Are you at mom and dad's? She and Journee there?" he asked.

He'd dropped Journee off with his parents the night

before. His family didn't want any excuses in the morning for him not getting on his flight.

"No, I'm at home and they went to the hospital to visit one of the deacons from the church. I told her I would check to make sure you got on that flight."

"She didn't take Journee to school?" he asked.

"She told me she was taking her in the afternoon because Journee had an appointment about a dance class she wanted to sign her up for and wasn't concerned about Journee missing a half-day of her pre-kindergarten day care class. She said she cleared it with you about dropping her off late today," Brynne said.

"Oh, I forgot. She did tell me about that."

He couldn't wait to see Journee in her new dance class. One of the reasons he decided to take the trip was so that he could find himself again and make sure he was the best father he could be to her. He had to stop living in the past as if his wife was going to one day walk through the door and everything in his life would go back to what it was supposed to be before the day of the accident that snatch everything away from him except for Journee. He smiled thinking about his daughter and what it took for her to actually be here which is how he came up with her name.

It took one hell of a journey for her to make an entrance in the world and survive even though, Peyton, his wife didn't survive her journey. He owed it to them both to be everything to Journee that she would need and the memory of Peyton is what pushed him to continue on day after day despite how much he missed her.

"Make sure you make the best of these days away and no work at all. That bank will be alright without your input. I want to hear all about this trip when you get back and none of it better involve some business deal you brokered while away. It better be filled with one excursion after another and maybe even some time with a fun lady to help pass the time. Get to the airport. I love you little brother."

Brody laughed. He would let her off the hook for now for slipping in the idea of him meeting a woman while on vacation. He wasn't ruling it out, but it wasn't first on his list. He was really looking forward to some down time and he couldn't think of a better place than a nice, warm island.

"You know I hate when you call me that. You're only a few minutes older than me," he said.

"I know and those few minutes mean I'm the oldest and I won't mention the better looking, but that's a given," Brynne laughed out loud.

"Love you, Brynne and I'll talk to you when I get back."

Now in the elevator, he rushed to get to the gym to change before rushing to his car to get to the airport. It was time for a new adventure and he had a feeling it was going to be found on the island of Turks and Caicos.

Chapter 4

"Oh, I needed that," Kimara said as she exited the bathroom after spending the last hour in the claw foot soaking tub. It was heavenly and she was more relaxed than she'd felt in a long time. She was now in her second full day on the island and she was already addicted to the tub.

Her clothes for the evening were laid out across the bed for an evening of fun and an attempt to be more outgoing. The night before, which was her first night on the island, she spent reading and enjoying the evening breeze as she sat outside on her veranda. She also enjoyed people watching as families enjoyed their time on the beach. Tonight, she was venturing out and looking forward to some fun with others.

Feeling extra sexy, she pulled out one of the tantalizing lace thong and demi-cup strapless bra sets in her favorite shade of royal blue. She was glad she let her sister talk her into a shopping spree for her trip in order for her to get some items she wouldn't normally pick for herself. She hadn't shopped for many things this sexy in a long time. There was a time in her life when she couldn't wait to hit the stores and pick up the sexiest lingerie she could find. Her heart or her head hadn't been in the game for a few years, but her sister was right, it was time for her to get out of her own way and get back to enjoying life and that meant finding her sexy again. Even if she didn't do it for the non-existent man in her life, she needed to do it for herself. It was time for her to rejoin the land of the living.

As for her dress, she chose a royal blue and white print, long flowing dress that was fitted in the top with thin straps. The strapless bra would go perfect with this dress, she thought as she skimmed over the eye-catching outfit. On her feet she decided on her favorite slinky, sling-back, strappy heels in the same shade of blue as the dress. Her plan was to get dressed later and rather than take the short path to the upcoming event for the night where all of the guests at the resort were invited to attend, she would get there by taking a stroll along the water edge on the beach.

Kimara couldn't wait to enjoy the crisp dark blue evening sky with her heels in her hand until she reached the party. For now, with a few hours before the party, she decided on a pair of shorts and a t-shirt so that she could do a little island shopping to pass the lazy day away. Slipping on a pair of flip-flops and briefly checking her make-up free face, she headed out. She had always been told that she had flawless skin and she loved that she didn't feel the need to cover it with a lot of make-up. She loved the natural beauty of her chestnut colored skin. Removing the shower cap, she let her hair flow down where it rested right above her shoulders in the back, but longer in the front. Her long, natural tresses didn't need a lot of work as she ran her fingers through it and managed to have it in place in seconds. She turned left and right to get a really good look at the bronze highlights that streaked throughout her naturally dark brown hair and loved how the color made her look and feel like a new woman. The new stylist did an incredible job on her new look. Gone was the dull, brown color that she'd been wearing for years, not giving it the attention it needed. Casey was right, it was time for some newness in her life. Time to grab that bull by the horn and find her niche again.

After locking the door to her villa, she took in the beautiful structure of the main walkway lined with beautiful paintings on the wall, while dynamic sculptured art graced the walkway. One of the sculpted pieces of a horse drew her attention. She had once dreamed of owning her very own farm where she could ride horses every day. That was a dream from years ago and until she saw the sculpture on her arrival, she hadn't thought much about it.

There were many dreams she'd buried long ago and she could kick herself for falling under a rock and living there away from life for the past five years. Inhaling, she took in a deep breath and loved the freshness in the air. It was a sign of the new freshness she was feeling about her life.

As she strolled through the hall toward the lobby, she passed by one store she would make sure to stop in before she left. It was a jewelry store and everything glittered like diamonds. First, she wanted to stop at the clothing store she remembered right off of the lobby. She loved shoes and remembered seeing a few in the window as she headed toward her room the day she checked in.

Almost to the lobby, she stopped in her tracks when her eyes settled on something or rather someone that took her breath away.

"Wow," Kimara said softly at the sight of a gorgeous

specimen of a man who stood talking to the staff member behind the main desk of their resort. Seeing him gave her system a sexy tinge as she eyed him from head to toe. What stood out first was the strong, determined way he stood. She imagined if Zeus, the Greek god actually existed, this is what he would look like. He was, at least, the image she had of him in the many books she read about Greek mythology. Not once in the past few years had she felt a tingling all over her body just at the sight of a man. Her focus was on his every move from the way he leaned down to sit his luggage down on the floor to the way he stood and rested his hands on the expansive check-in counter. This, she thought, was a man who was secure in everything about himself and it showed.

Suddenly she felt flushed and her hands felt clammy. She couldn't take her eyes off of him. She shocked herself at her immediate attraction to hm. She had dated some over the past few years, but nothing too serious. She hadn't met a man who made her think of dreamy, sexy nights until she set her eyes on the handsome specimen who was the current focus of all of her attention. He was drop dead gorgeous from his chestnut brown skin tone to the sexy goatee he sported and oh, did she love a man with a bald head. This man was herculean from his head to his feet and was dressed as if he'd just walked off of the cover of a men's fashion magazine. He wasn't in a suit, but was casually dressed in a sweat suit and even in that, he was the most stylish man she'd seen since she arrived.

Without realizing she was doing it, Kimara began fanning herself.

"Is this the kind of men that'll be walking around this place for the next few days," she said softly.

"Yes, girl!"

Kimara jumped at the sound of someone close by.

"I'm sorry, I didn't realize I'd said that out loud," she said, embarrassed that she'd spoken her thoughts out loud.

"It's okay. I understand where you're coming from. You aren't the only woman who noticed him. Take a look at all of the women in the lobby. I think they're all trying to figure out if he's coming or going. Don't be shy about it. If you're here on vacation, it's okay to indulge in a little fun and from the looks of that brother, I'd say he's more fun than any one man should ever exude."

"It's almost hypnotic, isn't it?" Kimara said.

"I met my husband here three years ago and we come back every year for our anniversary to remember the week we fell in love. I came here back then to have some fun with my friends and like the man who has captured all of your attention, I set eyes on my Larson and your look is a lot like the one I sported back then."

"Gorgeous, isn't he?" another woman said behind her.

Kimara was now officially embarrassed even more. Now, even more women knew she was secretly lusting over the man at the counter.

Kimara turned around to find three women ogling him as much as she was and to say she was mortified over her public display of desire for a man she didn't know, would be an understatement.

"Don't be ashamed at the thoughts running through your mind because we are all having a mutual experience imagining being up close and personal with all of that sexiness," another woman said.

"Nina and I flew in with him and I swear every woman on

the flight was in heat, including those who were married and tried hard to not let their husbands know they were checking him out. From what I can tell, he's not married or at least I didn't see a ring. He waited for the second shuttle while we got on the first one. We all watched him until he was out of sight and now here he is."

"I wonder if he's here for work or pleasure?" the first woman said.

Kimara had yet to respond to any of them and tried hard to not join in the conversation gawking at him like he was the last man on earth.

"Too bad I'm leaving today or I would do everything in my power to climb that hunk like I was a tree climber!" one of the other women said.

Kimara snickered at the visual and laughed along with the rest of them. They were like a group of she-devils and she no longer felt bad or guilty about checking him out so thoroughly.

"He is fine," Kimara finally said.

"Yes, he is," the others said together.

They all watched as a bellman took the man's luggage and they headed toward the villas on the opposite end of the resort. Secretly, Kimara hoped she would run into him again. She didn't know what had come over her, but the pull to see him again was strong. To think, she didn't come to the island to connect with a man, but it had been a lot of years since she'd had that type of instant attraction to any man and her body felt like it was on fire. She was instantly reminded that it had been five years since she'd been intimate with a man, yet her body was burning hot like a flow of heated lava in all the right places and all she did was get a glimpse of him.

"Maybe he'll be at the meet and greet party tonight. If he's here alone, can you imagine the women falling all over him?" one women said and Kimara laughed.

"Yeah, pretty much like we're all doing now," she laughed again. When the other ladies laughed, Kimara relaxed and felt a kinship with them already. There was no competition or hating over their equal admiration of the male specimen. The point was to know a good, hot looking man when you saw one and they had all seen him.

"Maybe he's meeting a woman here. Wouldn't that be something?" one said.

"Now, what woman wouldn't be holding on to him for dear life on this island of beautiful, sexy women? Wouldn't be me. I wouldn't let someone that sexy get far away from me."

Kimara thought the same, but didn't say it. She watched as the man followed the bellman toward the other end of the resort, most likely to his villa.

"Well, I guess this was a great welcome to the island for me. Nothing like checking out a sexy man," Kimara said and turned to the ladies.

"Speaking for myself here, I have no doubt if he set eyes on you, there would be no other woman taking his interest away. You are stunningly beautiful. I bet the minute he sees you, it's all over for any other woman here."

Kimara blushed as each woman shook their head in agreement.

"Thank you for the compliment, but I'm not here looking for a new man. I'm here to have some fun and relaxation for a few days," she admitted.

"Who said anything about a new man? I'm talking about

adding a man to your agenda of fun and relaxation for a few days. Trust me, I said the same thing and now I'm married to my island fling. Don't cut yourself short. Have some fun and return to your life back home. There is nothing wrong with enjoying your time here to the fullest," the woman who said she was married to someone named Larson that she'd met during a trip to this same resort stated.

Kimara hadn't thought a lot about how much enjoyment she would have when it came to the opposite sex on a romantic island like this. She knew people had rendezvous all the time in places like this and then went back to their normal lives afterward, never looking back. Could she be that risqué for once in her life?

"On this island, I'm sure men that look like him are a dime a dozen," Kimara said.

"True and you can have your pick. Well, I hope to see you at the party tonight and remember, this is paradise. Live in the moment and enjoy yourself. Just in case you didn't come prepared, the resort always provides a nice care package for travelers with everything you'll need. If not, your personal concierge can get you whatever you want. Have fun!"

Kimara waved as the women walked away and she looked in the direction the man had gone in. She could still see the back of him as he walked with determined long, bow-legged strides and her body again tingled at the sight of his sexy form as he walked away. There was something to be said about a sexy African American man. To her, there was none better.

Chapter 5

Brody couldn't get over the incredible villa that had been assigned to him for his stay. This particular resort had been recommended to him and so far, after just a few hours of being on the island, it definitely lived up to all of the hype.

His villa was a two-bedroom suite with all the amenities anyone could ask for. Remembering he filled out a questionnaire prior to his trip, he was happy to see that all of his wishes for his room were met. There was a television in each room and he even had a full kitchen since he loved to cook. He wasn't planning on doing a lot of cooking, but he liked the option if he chose to. The resort had food available all day and night that he could partake in, but after a few days, he may long for some of his own cooking.

He had a corner unit and therefore had an incredible view of the ocean on three sides. There was the capability to play music throughout the villa by connecting his phone or tablet to the system, something he specifically requested that reminded him of his own surround sound system at home. He loved everything about it and he hadn't even had a chance to venture outside yet. He had to admit that taking this short vacation was the best idea his friends had come up with in a long time.

He hadn't done much so far other than check out the room's amenities. He read up on various excursions he could sign up for and the package he had, each excursion was already included in the price for the trip his friends had gifted him. He was an adventurous and looked forward to deep sea diving, parasailing and going out on a boat for the day to enjoy the sun and experience the quietness of being out on the ocean.

All of the brochures about events were covered with photos of couples enjoying activities, but he was assured that each event was tailored for couples and for singles traveling alone. There were many opportunities to meet and connect with others on the island and to take advantage of everything that was offered. This was his first vacation in years and he was planning to make the most of it.

Finally unpacking his luggage after a few hours of relaxing and taking in the view, he felt a little out of pocket when his suitcase didn't include any work attire. He made a promise to his parents, sister and his friends that he would only take clothes to relax in since he was going to be spending a lot of time on the beach, which his mother pretty much demanded he do for five days.

The resort impressed him beyond any thought of what he assumed it would be like. One of the first things he noticed when he entered his villa was that he had direct access to the beach right off of the living room. Walking over to the sliding glass door, he opened it and the crisp air of the island and the fresh smell of the blue ocean greeted him. He remembered taking a look at the ocean earlier when the sun was high in the sky and noticing how blue the water was. That was something he didn't get to experience on beaches in the United States. He couldn't wait to check it out the next day. He was planning to get up and out early and hopefully find enough excitement that he would only spend time in his villa for sleeping.

Brody smiled and shook his head when he remembered what was waiting for him in his bedroom when he checked in. On the dresser in the bedroom was a bottle of wine, basket of fresh fruit and a box of all of the things his friends thought he would need for his stay on the island including a large box of condoms. The concierge had left the card that let him know his friends had sent the package to him. He chuckled at the conversation he and Nelson, his best friend had the day before he flew to the island.

He and Nelson Mancuso had been best friends since high school and Nelson had served as best man at his wedding to Peyton years ago. He and his wife, Amelia, had been a rock for him when Peyton died and as Journee's godparents, they had been by their side from day one of Journee's shaky entrance into the world.

He was thankful to them that they would help his mother and sister look after Journee while he was away for the week. He didn't like being away from his little angel, but everyone was correct when they told him he needed this time away and not just to wallow in remembrance of the day he lost Peyton, but to learn how to live again and not just focus on work and raising Journee.

Leave it to Nelson, he thought, to send him wine, fruit and a box of what he called essentials for being on an island where some of the sexiest women were known to vacation and live. He would love to say he was on an adventure to sow some wild oats before returning home, but that wasn't first on his list. That wasn't a need he didn't fulfill when he needed to back at home, so he wasn't in search of something he wasn't already indulging in. He did surprise himself that he wasn't involved on a more long-term basis with a woman. He loved being married and loved the connection that could be made with the right person, but for him, he wasn't sure he was ready for anything more than casual nights with women who knew the score going in when it came to how involved he would be with them.

He loved women and thought of how lovely they all were in their own way. He enjoyed hanging out with friends at events and meeting beautiful women. He never brought any to the home he shared with his daughter, making sure to keep his home life and his private life separate. Nelson once referred to him as a player on the rise when they talked about the casualness of his dating life, but he didn't see it that way. Brody saw nothing wrong with two people satisfying a craving without any type of serious commitment that neither were ready for.

He agreed that men and women were different in how they saw things when it came to relationships. While men were more visual, women entered into relationships with men leading with their heart. It's how they were created to be. He was happy that the women he'd connected with were living lives as busy as his and only had time for casual flings, which suited him fine.

What he would do with his time on the island he hadn't yet thought through. If he found a woman who was interested in an island fling for a few days, he wouldn't turn it down as long as they agreed what happens on the island, stays on the island and that they will put it behind them when it was time to go back to their lives. After all, it was all a part of the getaway to a sexy island experience.

Going back into the bedroom to finish unpacking the last remnants of his luggage, he pulled out his own stash of condoms he'd brought along just in case. He was a man who was always prepared just in case. He was not one who was shy about his sexual prowess and from the women he encountered on his flight here to those he spotted as he entered the resort, to say there were some beautiful women here would be an understatement.

First and foremost, he was preparing for a night of fun and getting to know others who were on the island by attending the meet and greet his first night on the island. From what he was told about it, there would be lots of food, dancing and just all-around fun for the entire night. He could use a night out to keep his mind on the reason for getting away and not on the event five years ago that drastically changed his life. Peyton would want him to get back to living his life. She wouldn't be proud that he hadn't found another woman to love and live for as he had with her and wasn't sure he ever would. His life was about raising Journee and making sure he was there for whatever she wanted and needed. His time for him was secondary.

As the sun began to go down, Brody knew he should be preparing for the party, but the beautiful sunset drew his attention. The party was just beginning and he didn't mind being a little late if he could spend a little time checking out what a sunset looked like on an island as beautiful as Turks and Caicos.

He walked out onto his private patio and looked up at the night sky, knowing that the calmness of the evening is exactly what he needed for his time away. At home, he never took time to enjoy peace and quiet. There was always a work issue he needed to tend to and that included extremely late hours. For a chance, he could focus on something else entirely.

When he should be leaning back and enjoying the beautiful sight, a much more beautiful and incredible sight garnered his attention. In the far-left corner of his eye, a vision so magnificent came across his view and for a moment, nothing else mattered.

With the sun rushing to set and the glow of the remainder of daylight mixed with the most beautiful scene of his life, Brody wasn't sure he wasn't asleep and dreaming. Do men really dream of women this beautiful?

Before him and coming full center with his view of the beach was a woman so stunning, she took his breath away. There wasn't any one thing that drew him in; it was everything. It was the way she walked and enjoyed the night air as if she didn't have a care in the world. It was the way she walked slowly along the beach taking her time to let the sand flow through her toes with each step. It was the way her long hair flowed in the slight breeze blowing through the trees on the edge of the beach. It was the long, flowing dress that blew in the wind all around her body. He couldn't see her face, but he didn't need to because there was an aura about her that said everything and unlike any other time in his life, with any other woman, he felt drawn to her and the freedom that she brought with her as she walked along the beach. Who was she?

She appeared to be walking in the direction of the party which reminded him of where he needed to be. For now, he couldn't take his eyes off of the woman who screamed out at him with all of her magnificent beauty even though she didn't know it. For the first time in his life, a woman at a distance had him enraptured. He stood and leaned forward over the railing and followed her every move. To someone watching him, he looked like a stalker, but to him, he was a man enchanted by her essence and his body immediately hardened. It wasn't a hardening of his most intimate body part, but his body as a whole. He was ready to sprint down the walkway from his patio to catch up with her, not wanting to let her get away without learning everything he could about her.

What kind of woman has this kind of impact on a man? His mind raced as his body steeled and thoughts ran rampant through his mind of having her in his arms and telling her of all of the beautiful things he thought about the minute he set eyes on her. Was she an islander? A visitor on vacation? Was she on the island alone, with friends or perhaps with a male guest? If she was in fact going to the party, there was only one way to find out and he needed to know. Everything in him said this woman was someone he would not want to let get away. He shook as it seemed as if the night breeze blowing by his ear was speaking to him and telling him she is a woman who won't soon forget.

Now focused, he knew he needed to get a shower, change and head to the party.

As he made his way to the shower, he couldn't help but replay the image of the woman walking alone on the private villa beach and longed to see her again. If fate were having a hand in his time away, it just placed him on his patio at the exact moment the most exquisite woman in the world had walked by and to him, that was all he needed invigorate him even more about his time on the island. It was time to go have some fun.

Chapter 6

Walking on shaky legs, Kimara walked closer to the area where music was playing and people could be heard laughing and having a good time. While she walked along the beach to the event, she wondered how many women were on the island alone without a male counterpart like her. Throughout the day, the thought hadn't occurred to her how awkward it would be if she attended the event and found a room full of couples.

Now that she was actually here, she looked around at several groups of women, men and couples and exhaled her relief. She wasn't the only person attending stag for the evening. The last thing she wanted to do was stick out like a sore thumb.

Walking up to the entrance, she handed her ticket to the event to one of the two men collecting them and after giving her instructions of where she could get a drink, she was handed a name tag and entered the main room. A level of comfort came over her instantly as she saw people milling about, laughing, dancing and having a good time. As she walked around, everyone greeted her and conversed as if they had been long lost friends.

The music was loud and lively and she could already feel her hips begin to sway to the sound of the live band who were jamming to the tunes of Earth, Wind & Fire, one of her favorite old-school groups.

The smell of delicious cuisine made her stomach growl and she couldn't wait to dive in. She knew women often curtailed their appetites in the presence of large groups, but she was a foodie and loved not being shy about the way she dived right into foods she enjoyed. The fact that she loved working out and kept in good shape, she didn't mind indulging every now and then.

Looking around, she saw some familiar faces from earlier in the day and when they waved her over to their table, she walked over, thankful she wouldn't have to sit at an empty table waiting for someone friendly to join her. After exchanging names and hellos around the table, she joined the conversation and before long, she was laughing and even got in a few dances and partook in a glass of her favorite non-alcoholic drink, strawberry daiquiri. Not being one to drink more than a single glass of wine, she chose to keep her week on the island alcohol free for the most part around an island full of people she didn't know. She wanted to remain in control of all of her faculties.

"Are you having a great time on the island?" Jessica asked her. Kimara had finally gotten the name of the woman she'd met earlier in the lobby who had met her husband on this very island a few years back by looking at her name tag.

"I am. I haven't had this much fun in a long time. Thanks for inviting me to join your table."

"No problem. I was looking out for you. I remember you

saying you were planning to attend. This gathering is held every other night and it's always fun."

"You sound like a pro at being at the resort," Kimara said.

"It's our favorite of all of them. How are you settling in to your villa? Nice isn't it?" Jessica said.

"Yes, it is. I had no idea it would be that fantastic. I lounged in that claw foot tub last night and earlier today and I hated having to get out," she said.

"You'll find you're going to feel that way about everything here. Did you get the chance to do any sightseeing yet?" Jessica asked.

"Not really. Nothing besides checking out the gorgeous men I spotted while I did some shopping earlier. Is that the norm because every man was hotter than the last," she said laughing.

"You noticed that too, huh? A lot of people come here to escape the crazy life they have at home and a lot of those people are sexy, hot, gorgeous men. Remember the guy from earlier in the lobby? I think I saw him a few minutes ago. It's crowded in here now and I'm not one hundred percent sure it's him, but it's a strong possibility. Are you thinking of indulging in a little male fun while you're here? If so, there's nothing wrong with that."

Kimara hadn't thought a whole lot about that, but she would remain open to whatever her week provided and she would approach whatever she does, cautiously. She couldn't imagine a desire so strong that she would do it considering it had been five years for her, but she never said never. Maybe she would be open to having some island fun to get back on the horse, as her sister would say.

"I don't know. I'm not saying no and there is definitely the potential to indulge in some island fun. I guess time will tell."

Kimara waited as long as she could before checking out the crowd as her eyes searched for the mystery man from the lobby she's spotted earlier in the day. There were hundreds of good looking men around and some appeared to be single, but something in her told her she only wanted to see the man from earlier in the day. There was a strong desire to see him again and it wasn't simply because she felt a zing through her body that she hadn't experienced in a long time.

"Larson and I are going back out on the dance floor," Jessica said standing.

"Have fun. I'm going to grab a few more of those delicious shrimp and maybe one more daiquiri," Kimara said standing with them. She made her way over to the large buffet in the back of the room.

**

The crowd was large by the time he reached the event and Brody took his time making his way through the crowd on the dance floor. Catching a whiff of the as a reminder that he'd had nothing to eat, his stomach growled at the thought of getting something in it. He walked around a bit and even danced for a few brief moments with a woman who pulled him onto the dance floor without even asking. He went with the flow and danced until hunger pains took over. He thanked her for the dance and headed towards the food buffet. He'd find a table to sit down at after getting a sample of the food.

As soon as he reached the table, he struggled with where to start. Everything looked delicious from the lobster tails, to the braised steak fillets with small potatoes. Looking down the table, he spotted so many delicacies, he realized he wasn't just hungry – he was starving.

After piling a few items onto his plate to start out with, the sight of one of his favorite foods, stuffed shrimp, caught his eye. Seeing that there were only two left, he reached for them and encountered another hand that was reaching for the same thing. Drawing his hand back and all set to apologize, the words were caught in his throat as the most strikingly beautiful woman smiled at him. He could see that she was about to say something, but like him, words would not come out. Brody couldn't stop staring and, in a minute, he would officially be ogling her.

"I'm sorry," he finally said as words formed in his brain.

"No, I'm sorry. I didn't realize you were reaching for the shrimp, too. Since there are only two, why don't you take them."

Brody was a goner. Who was this woman and should he tell her he was already in love with her? The way she talked, smiled and the gentleness in her demeanor spoke volumes. He smiled and inwardly laughed at himself. He wasn't serious, but if he were, he knew he would be over the moon with happiness. Still staring, there was something familiar about her, but he couldn't put his finger on it.

"Oh, no, ladies first. I'm sure there will be more since the party will run late into the night. I heard the buffet stays stocked as long as people are here enjoying the party," he said.

Kimara almost lost the ability to say anything else when realization struck her. Standing in front of her, talking about shrimp was the man she'd been gawking over in the lobby a few hours earlier. There was no way he could get any more handsome than he had been earlier, but he just had. When he smiled at her, her heart practically leaped out of her chest. Relaxing her beating heart, she returned the smile.

"Are you sure? Why don't we each take one and then make a dash to the table when we see more?" Kimara said as they both broke out into a fit of laughter.

"Good idea."

Brody signaled for her to take hers first and then he reached for the one left over.

"Thank you," Kimara said and turned when the person behind her grumbled at the shrimp being gone.

Brody leaned in closer to her.

"I guess we better stake out this table. It's clear the shrimp are the hit of the night. If they put more out and I'm able to snag a few, I'll grab some for you, too," he said and hoped his attempt at flirting, something he was rusty at, wasn't coming on too strong. Everything in him said his bumping into her was no coincidence, especially since he couldn't seem to stop staring at her.

Kimara laughed out loud again.

"I'll tell you what, you have my back and I'll have yours," she said.

Brody didn't want to say she wouldn't need to because he was already watching everything about her. His stalk-like behavior didn't stop as he watched her walk away in the direction of a table on the other side of the room. He saw a table not far from hers that had a few empty seats and he headed in that direction.

As he sat down, he looked at the woman again and there was a certain familiarity that he couldn't shake. Did he know her? Perhaps she was on the same flight he was on coming to the island. Whoever she was, she was incredibly beautiful and in that long flowing dress, she was a dynamic beauty. Wait, he thought. I can't be. Is it her?

Before he could focus on his thoughts, a voice over the speaker system interrupted him as everyone turned in the direction of the speaking voice.

"Ladies and gentlemen, welcome to tonight's meet and greet. We hope everyone has a great time mingling and getting to know each other. The music will continue as long as people are still here, the food will flow all night long and drinks will be poured until no one orders another one. Thankfully, no one has to drive and each of your villas are within walking distance. The only people allowed here tonight are guests of this resort, so feel safe knowing that there are no outsiders who have not been vetted by us very carefully. Please wear your name tags all night long and we hope you meet some people who will become instant friends. If you need help getting back to your villa or would feel more comfortable having an escort to make sure you are safely inside, please don't hesitate to let one of our hostesses know. Have fun and intermittently, we'll interrupt with a fun game or activity which is meant to make sure you have a great time during your stay here at Grace Bay on the island of Turks and Caicos."

After everyone clapped, the band started playing and the dance floor became crowded once again. He could now turn his attention back to the woman knowing why she seemed familiar to him. He watched her get up and head for the dance floor and the way her dressed moved around her as she swayed, he had no doubt she was the woman he'd seen a while ago walking along the beach outside of his villa. He tried to remember the name from the tag on her chest, but had to admit to himself, he was too busy focusing on her beauty and that incredibly sexy body to have really focused on her name. He did remember it was something with the letter "K".

He watched her as she danced and the way she moved, he couldn't take his eyes off of her. She moved with so much life and enjoyment and her free spirit spread out over the room like a quiet, loving embrace. Brody knew that she was dancing with someone and he hoped he wouldn't be out of place if he interrupted and asked her for a dance. Pushing his plate to the side, he stood just as she was leaving the dance floor and heading to the buffet table. This was his chance to talk to her again, he thought, as he headed in the same direction. Brody felt like his destiny was waiting for him there.

Chapter 7

"We meet again and this time we don't have to tussle for the last piece of shrimp," Brody said as he came up to stand before the world's most beautiful woman.

"I'm glad I didn't have to use my karate skills on you over some shrimp. That could have gotten pretty ugly," Kimara countered and laughed along with him.

Checking out his name tag, she saw that his name was Brody, a name she had a feeling she wasn't going to be able to forget.

"I wouldn't want that," Brody said.

"Well, thank you for not hurting me in the name of shrimp. I have to admit, that one shrimp I had wasn't enough and now that I see there's a large tray full, I say we're both going to be safe from injury."

Brody laughed out loud.

"That wouldn't be a good look for me in this room full of people, Kimara," he said looking at her name tag. "You have a beautiful name," he added.

"Thank you and I have a feeling any look on you wouldn't be a bad one, Brody" she said boldly as she checked out his name tag and then had to think twice about who just said the words that came out of her mouth. This island already had her acting unlike herself. If she didn't know any better, she would say she just flirted with a complete stranger on an exotic island.

"After you eat your fill of shrimp this go 'round, would I be too forward if I asked you to dance?" he asked, feeling hopeful.

Kimara tried to hold her excitement back since she had been hoping he would ask her. She wasn't sure she could gather up another bold bone in her body to ask him, even though she wanted nothing more at the moment than to dance with him.

"Not at all. I would love, too. In fact, knowing the shrimp tray will be filled again and again, if you'd like to dance right now, I'd be up for it," she said.

"Are you sure? I know you just left the dance floor."

"I'm sure. Are you up for it? I wouldn't want to make you look bad or anything with my incredible dance moves," Kimara said, jokingly.

Brody extended his hand to her.

"Take your best shot, beautiful," he said. When she placed her hand in his, his first thought was to move toward the dance floor, but he was stopped cold in his tracks when he felt a tingle that zapped right through him, traveling from his hand where it grasped hers, all the way through his body. He turned toward her and knew the feeling he felt had touched her as well. Now wasn't the time to address it, but already, he felt a strong, unwavering connection to her.

Reaching the center of the floor, he started moving to the fast beat and when he turned toward her, she was giving him a run or his money. They were magic together and when he looked around, others were marveling at their dance moves.

For three songs in a row, they moved with and against each other rhythmically as if it were not the first time they had danced together. They seemed to be in perfect sync until a break in the music came as another person began talking in the microphone. As the dance floor began to clear, he took her by the hand to walk her over to the table where he saw her sitting earlier. When they reached her table, he pulled out her chair and leaned down when he saw her speaking to him.

"I have not danced like that in a long time," Kimara said taking a seat.

"Me either. You're a great dancer. Thanks for dancing with me," he said.

"So are you. Would you like to sit down? There's an extra seat at our table unless you have another place you'd prefer sitting. I don't want to keep you from someone else" she said.

"There is no one else you're keeping me from and I'd love to join you," Brody said pulling out the chair next to her and sitting down.

For the next hour, through the sound of loud music, laughter and partying, Brody enjoyed talking to Kimara and hearing about how much she was already enjoying the island. They had been so indulged in each other, that neither noticed the crowd had begun thinning out.

"I guess it's getting pretty late," Kimara said as she looked around.

"Do you realize we've been sitting here talking for over an hour?" Brody said looking at the time.

"Has it been an hour?" she asked.

"Yes, and it is very late."

As if on cue, Kimara let out a big yawn and was about to apologize when Brody laughed.

"Are you ready to leave? Looks like I may be boring you," he quipped.

"I am so sorry. Trust me, you are far from boring. I've enjoyed talking to you. I guess I am a little tired and still a little jetlagged," she said.

"I could walk you back to your villa or if you would prefer, there is security here that could make sure you got back safely. I have to admit, I would enjoy your company on the walk back," he said.

Kimara looked into Brody's handsome face and without openly saying so, she wasn't happy that the evening was already ending. Once they started talking, she couldn't get enough of hearing his deep baritone voice as he spoke so eloquently. Once the words went from his lips to her ears, her entire body burned with titillating anticipation. Of what, she didn't know, but his voice wreaked havoc on her senses. She couldn't chalk it up to alcohol because she hadn't drunk anything all night. The man was nothing but pure magnetism.

"I would enjoy your company as well. Are you sure you don't mind? I know it's pretty late," she said.

"I don't mind at all. What kind of gentleman would I be after taking up your time this evening and not making sure you got back safely. Is there anyone with you that we should wait for?" he asked.

"No. The others at the table were some new friends I met when I got here and they were gracious enough to invite me to sit with them tonight. I'm ready whenever you are," she said and stood.

Extending his hand, Brody smiled when she placed her small hand into his larger one. As soon as she stood, he saw a look on her face that said there was an issue with her feet which probably stemmed from the full night of dancing they had done.

"I would love the company, but if you don't mind, I'd like to walk along the beach back to my room. If I were alone, I would go the safest route, but I have a feeling no one would bother me if I'm with you. That way I can take these shoes off and carry them. Not all shoes are made for the amount of dancing I did tonight," Kimara admitted.

He smiled gleefully.

"A walk along the beach edge it is, but first, hand me those shoes on your feet. The sand will feel good and relaxing to your feet. I recognized that look on your face when you stood. My sister sports the same look when I'm out with her and her feet have coughed and died on her," Brody joked.

Kimara smiled and exhaled. No need in trying to hide the obvious. The shoes were cute, but were killing her feet.

"Yeah, that's pretty much where I am right now. I love to dance, but these shoes were made to be cute and not to be danced in for hours."

Brody leaned down close to her ear. "Trust me, you nailed the cuteness factor," he said.

Kimara reached down to pull off her shoes. Removing both, she smiled when he reached for them. She didn't think he was serious about carrying them.

"You don't have to carry my shoes," she said.

"Of course, I do. I feel responsible since I kept asking you to dance and being the great dancer that I am, you couldn't resist every single time," he smiled happily.

"You are a great dancer."

"A compliment from another great dancer just made my night. Should we get going," he said reaching for her shoes again.

This time Kimara handed him her heels and took the elbow he extended to her.

"Have a good night you two!"

Kimara and Brody turned around and said good night to one other couple that was still sitting at their table. They had talked to them throughout the night and being good at remember names, Brody thanked them.

"Paul and Constance, right?" he asked.

"Yes, and you're Brody and she's Kimara, right?" Constance said.

Kimara and Brody both nodded.

"It was a pleasure sharing the evening and a table with you. My wife and I are here for a few more days and it was fun being table mates with you. We're planning to do a few excursions tomorrow, deep-sea diving, water skis and a few more things if you both would like to join us? We were hoping to meet some other couples to do some fun things with while we were here. Jessica and Larson who were here are planning to join us, too."

Brody and Kimara looked back and forth at each other. The couple thought that they were a couple, too.

"Oh, we're not a couple. We just met here tonight," Kimara said.

"Really? The way the two of you moved together and looked at each other, we thought we were looking at a couple in love. Well, the invitation still stands if you want to connect, we're planning to get up early enough for the brunch buffet and if you want to join us for the water skis, meet us at the buffet and we'll go from there. There are a few other activities we could do while our food digests before deep sea diving. There are brochures all over the place. If not, we hope to see you again before we leave," Constance said.

Brody didn't want to answer for Kimara, but he would love to spend the day with her so that he could get to know even more about her. The fact that another couple sensed something between them solidified his thoughts that Kimara was about to become someone special. The idea shocked him since he'd just met her. The vision of her walking along the beach earlier stood out in his mind and the memory of the instant attraction to her came flooding back. What that coupled sensed was real and he had a feeling Kimara knew it, too. He didn't want to waste any time to see if she was just as interested in spending more time with him as he was with her.

"I'm open to hanging with you guys if Kimara is okay with it. I haven't signed up for anything yet and from the brochure, it looks like there is a lot to do here. Are you adventurous?" he asked her.

Kimara smile, overjoyed that he would be interested in spending more time with her.

"I came here to enjoy myself and not stay closed up in my villa, so yeah, I'm adventurous if you are," she responded.

"Sounds like you'll be meeting us for brunch which will be here before you know it," Paul said.

"We'll see you in a few hours," Constance said standing along with her husband. She walked close to Kimara and whispered in her ear. "I really thought you were a couple in love. Something is happening and I like it."

Though Brody was sure Constance was trying to whisper, he heard every word.

Looking at each other again, neither said a word, but waved to Constance and Paul as they left. She looked around and didn't see Jessica and Larson or the other ladies who were at the table. She assumed they had already left for the evening. She knew that she would soon get a huge smile from Jessica once she saw her and Brody together in the morning. She will remember him from the lobby and all the ogling they were doing.

"They really thought we were a couple," Kimara said turning to walk with Brody toward the beach.

"Well, tonight we were and that's okay with me," he admitted.

Silence ensued as they walked out of the rear entrance along the path that lead to the sandy beach. Like two familiar lovers, they walked hand in hand and neither made a gesture to let go. Kimara had a feeling the instant attraction she felt for him was mutual and neither of them were fighting it. She waited as Brody removed his own shoes the moment they reached the sand.

She wanted to know more about Brody. As they talked at the table, he shared with her that he worked as a vice president for a bank and was in need of a vacation from everyday life. She also learned that like the activities they would be taking part in the next morning, he loved adventure and all things around being active. That clearly showed by how in shape he was. She couldn't help checking out his tone physique as they danced and knew without actually seeing it that he didn't have an ounce of fat on his body. She wouldn't be surprised if he worked out every day, something she herself had gotten in the habit of doing and loved.

Though he was tall, over six feet and strappingly strong, the way he held her hand was soft and affectionate. Oh, what a man, she thought and wondered how many questions would be too many. She didn't want to borderline prying into his personal life. She didn't know if he wanted to keep that part of his life to himself. Then again, she would never know if she didn't ask.

"So, no wife or girlfriend back at home waiting for you who would mind that another couple thought you were involved with a woman on the island?" she asked and waited to see if he was hesitant in responding. When he looked over at her as they walked and smiled, her nervousness over prying eased up.

"There is no one back home staking claim to be besides my soon to be five-year-old daughter and of course my twin sister who loves acting as much like my mother as my mother does. As far as anyone close, the answer is no. What about you? Am I violating the bro-code? Is there a man in your life that I may have to challenge to a duel for your attention?" he joked.

"None at all and for some reason, I wish there was just so that I could see this duel," she laughed.

"Listen, the little I know about you and how beautiful I know you are, I have a feeling the duel would be worth the reward of winning your hand and possibly a date? I know we're hanging out with some people tomorrow during the day, but I'm hoping I can convince you to have dinner with me tomorrow night," Brody said, hopeful.

"Dinner would be nice and I would love to. This island is absolutely gorgeous. Even though the evening is hot, the sand is cool under my feet."

"Yes, it is and I guess that's why people call this paradise. It's felt like that since the moment I got off the plane. I can't begin to tell you how much I needed this getaway," he said.

"So did I. I'm glad I came," Kimara said.

"I'm glad you did, too," Brody said looking over at her and locking eyes. He shocked himself at the instant affection and not just attraction he was feeling. Truly a first for him from someone he'd just met.

He was more than glad she took the trip to the island and was even happier she did so during the same week that he was here.

"That's my villa right over there," Kimara pointed out.

Reaching the gate to her villa, she took out her card key, needed for entrance into this part of the resort. Before going inside, she turned back to him since their hands were still locked in a grip.

"I hope you had a great time tonight," Brody said.

"I had the best time tonight and thank you for being a part of it."

"I look forward to seeing you in a few hours."

Kimara smiled knowing that's how she felt, too.

"Try not to oversleep," she said.

"Nothing will make me miss the chance to spend more time with you. I'll see you at the buffet. Go ahead inside. I want to be sure the lock clicks before I leave," he said handing her shoes to her.

Kimara walked a few steps before turning back around.

"I have to admit something to you, if that's okay," she said.

"Sure, anything."

"I saw you earlier in the day when you were checking in. I was standing near a jewelry store off of the lobby and you walked in. I'm almost ashamed to say I was ogling you from a distance and I hoped I would see you tonight at the meet and greet," he boldly admitted. She was out of character and in rare form, but a presence was nudging her to share her thoughts.

"Well, I hope I held up to your expectation of meeting me in person," Brody said.

"That and then some," Kimara admitted.

"Well, since we're admitting things. When I saw you at the party, I remembered you from a few hours ago, too. I was sitting on my patio taking in the sunset and I saw this beautiful woman in a blue and white flowing dress as she walked along the beach and the sight of her took my breath away. All I could think was that I needed to meet her. Once I got to the party and saw you, I knew you were the woman from the beach," he said.

Kimara smiled up at Brody and realized they both had the same reaction to each other without the other person knowing it.

"That was me. I wanted to stroll along the water's edge before it got too dark. You saw me?" she asked.

"I did and if weren't for the fact that I didn't want to be seen as some stalker, I would have come after you to meet you at that moment. I figured you were heading to the party or at least I really hoped you were. What do you think about the word, fate?" he said.

Kimara nodded, thinking the same thing.

"I think it's a great word," she said. "I'll see you soon?" she asked.

"Yes, you will. Once you're inside, cut a light on so that I know the door is locked behind you before I let the gate here close," he said.

Brody watched her walk away and his heart began pumping wildly in his chest. This was more than just your basic attraction to a woman. He knew it was much more than that.

After waiting a few seconds, he saw her light go on and he let the gate close and lock. Checking that it was secure, he walked in the direction of his room. He had no doubt, the rest of his night would be filled with thoughts of Kimara. He'd met his woman from the beach and she was all he knew she would be. If there was such a thing as love at first sight, he knew he'd just experienced it. He knew he needed to slow his thoughts down because he had only spent a few hours with her, but deep down inside, that thought was not going to change. He'd just fallen in love at first sight.

Chapter 8

"Kimara! Over here."

Kimara looked in the direction of where her name was being called and spotted Jessica, her husband and the other couple from their table. Looking around, she didn't see Brody anywhere and wondered if he'd changed his mind.

"Good morning!" she exclaimed excitedly. She didn't want to let on that she was disappointed that she didn't see Brody at the table. She knew she was running a little behind after sleeping a little later than planned after having a crazy time falling asleep as thoughts of Brody kept her awake.

No man had ever had that instant awareness kind of impact on her, enough to keep her up at night thinking about him after meeting him only a few hours before. She kept thinking over the few things he shared about himself with her and his sexy lips and handsome face kept her wide awake.

She knew that he loved his family, especially his daughter. He didn't say anything about her mother and whether they still had any kind of connection and from the way he only mentioned his daughter, parents, sister and best friend, she figured if he wanted to bring her up, he would have. Once he told her he didn't have a significant other waiting for him back home, that was all she needed to know.

He had shared that he was in banking and that outside of working, most of his time was spent with his daughter. She loved how he talked about her and all of the fun things they did together. She could tell he loved her very much. She felt a tinge of jealousy wishing she'd had a child to love the way Brody loved his daughter. It hadn't been in the cards for her. She also hoped what she and Brody mutually felt wasn't just for the night before. She felt a connection like never before and was looking forward to getting to know even more.

"We're glad you could make it. We still have some time before the first excursion. We weren't sure you were still coming," Constance said.

"Looks like Brody may have changed his mind. I don't see him anywhere," she said, looking around once again.

"You mean that sexy hunk from the lobby we saw and the same man you danced with for the rest of the night? I mean the way the two of you were into each other, it was like no one else was in the room. I'm glad you finally got the chance to meet him," Jessica said.

"Well, I'm not sure what happened this morning. I was sure he wanted to go out on a few excursions this morning," Kimara said. She would have rung his room except for the fact that she didn't have his last name and didn't know his villa number. That information was needed before the resort would dial his room.

"Your *McSexy* has already been here," Constance said.

"Did he leave?" she asked immediately and then she felt embarrassed at being that excited.

"No. He said he was going to sign the two of you up for the same excursions we signed up for. When we got here this morning, Constance told us you would be joining us and Larson held two more spots for you two and Brody went to confirm them. He didn't want to lose the spots knowing they needed a name to hold them.

What a relief, she thought. Kimara shouldn't have doubted what she knew the two of them were feeling the night before. Now that she knew he was in fact ready for the day, she needed to grab some food in order to catch up with everyone else.

"I'm going to grab a bite to eat," she said walking away.

When she reached the brunch buffet, the food looked even more delightful than it had the night before. There was an array of breakfast and lunch items and a station that was prepared to make any kind of omelet to order. After grabbing some fruit and a cup of coffee, she walked over to the omelet station and got in line behind two other people.

"Starting without me?"

Kimara's skin sizzled at the sound of Brody's deep voice right next to her ear. Inwardly, she trembled and hoped her reaction to him wasn't as evident to him as it was to her. The man's voice did sexy things to her body.

She turned around and smiled.

"Good morning. I'm glad to see you didn't oversleep," she said.

"And miss a day with you? Not on your life. You look amazing."

Kimara blushed knowing it took her almost an hour to decide what to wear. She decided on a pair of light blue shorts and a thin white top. Underneath, she had on a one-piece navy and white bathing suit. She had also remembered to bring a bag with a change of clothes in case hers were soaked by the time they got back.

"Thank you. I see you dress down quite nicely," she said checking him out. Before her stood her exact image of a god in person. This morning, he was wearing a short sleeved gray shirt and black shorts. The night before, he'd had on long pants, but this morning, his legs were on display and the moment she looked down at them, her mouth watered. How could a man exude this much potent sexuality, she thought? As she remembered from the night before, she knew he was someone who worked out and his perfectly toned legs, looking all muscular and sexy were perfection. She was having a hard time understanding how he couldn't have a woman at home waiting or one in his life in general. No way could any woman pass up on a man as gorgeous as Brody was.

"Thank you. I woke up ready for the day to begin," he said.

"I'm grabbing an omelet and there's a full layout of food over there. Have you already eaten?" she asked.

"No. As soon as I got here, our new friends told me about the hold on the excursions and I didn't want to lose them. Are you okay with parasailing, deep-sea diving and a day out on a boat? Those seem to be the most popular with the group."

"Those sound perfect. I've never done any of them, but I love the water and I'm a great swimmer. Sounds like a great day to me. Thanks for making sure we didn't lose our spots," she said.

"Even if we had, I would have found something else for us to do. I'm looking more forward to doing the activities with you than the actual activities," he said.

"So am I," Kimara said, blushing once again. Oh, the feelings the man sent through her with his presence.

"I'm going to grab some food from the buffet. Can I pick up anything or you?" Brody asked.

"No, I picked up a few things and took them back to the table already. Would you like me to order you an omelet? I see the line behind me is getting long."

"Sure. If you don't mind, I'd love a Spanish omelet."

"Spanish omelet it is. I'll bring it with me back to the table," she said.

"I'll be there waiting."

Kimara knew is she could see her face in a mirror, she would look like a school girl having a crush on the most popular body. She felt all girlie and loved it.

After Brody walked off, it was Kimara's turn to order. She waited to the side while their food was being prepared. Her eyes found Brody at the table and she couldn't look away. She also noticed several other pairs of eyes focused on him. One woman even looked her way and gave her the thumbs up. She couldn't stifle the giggle that rose up in her throat. She had to admit they did look good together. A few more days on the island and she was excited to see what the rest of her time would provide. Time with Brody, she hoped.

**

"Are you having a good time?" Brody asked coming up to sit next to Kimara as she lay out in the sun on the back of the motor yacht they'd rented for the afternoon. After the fun of the first two excursions, the final activity was a quiet ride on the yacht they'd rented and everyone was quietly enjoying being out on the water. Now clad in black swimming trunks while Kimara comfortably relaxed in a one-piece suit that had his body doing all kinds of flips, he settled in next to her while setting a plate of fresh fruit between them.

"I'm having a wonderful time. This is one of the best days of my life. I never thought I'd go deep-sea diving and I would absolutely do it again. What about you? Enjoying your time out today?" she asked.

"This day has been everything to me and spending it with you has made it even more pleasurable. Besides, seeing you in this bathing suit is well worth the day with you. You are incredibly beautiful, something I'm sure you know."

"Thank you for the compliment."

"Still interested in dinner with me tonight?" he asked.

"Absolutely. I'm looking forward to it."

"Great. I made reservations at a restaurant that came highly recommended by the resort manager. So, am I prying if I ask what the motivation behind was taking a vacation to this island alone?" Brody asked. They haven't had much time to really talk because they'd been having so much fun swimming and then parasailing. Now, with a little down time, he wanted to know more.

"Sure. I went through something tragic a few years ago and each year I found myself focusing too much on the tragedy. This year, I wanted to do something different to celebrate how important it is to embrace life and enjoy every minute of it."

"I can relate to that. Our reasons are similar and I must say meeting you has been a highlight of my stay here. I'd love to get to know even more about you. While everyone is enjoying some down time while out here, what do you say we play a speed game of getting to know you?" Brody asked.

Kimara was intrigued. She would like nothing more than to know and share more. She was already fascinated by him after a full day of seeing him in action.

"Sure. How do we play this game?" she asked.

"Well, I'll say two words and you respond by saying which one is more you and then you get to do the same. We also get to answer what we ask. We get to find out our likes and dislikes. Up for it?" he asked.

"Sounds fun."

"Okay, I'll start."

"Ice cream – chocolate or vanilla?"

"Vanilla," Kimara said.

"Vanilla for me, too. Thanks to my daughter, we eat it covered it sprinkles."

"Okay, my turn for one. Coffee or tea?" she asked.

"Definitely coffee. When I think of tea, I think of little ol' ladies sipping tea with their pinkies in the air," Brody joked.

"You mean you don't play tea party with your daughter?" Kimara asked.

Brody laughed out loud, not expecting that and remembering his most recent tea party with Journee and how she forced him to dress up and even put barrettes in his hair and pink polish on his finger nails. He knew he would do anything for her, including play dress-up.

"Well, in that instance, we fake drinking tea and yeah, we have tea parties at least once a week. Please don't ask me what else I'm forced to do at those tea parties. Let's just say my daughter is very demanding and has a pretty girly creative side," he quipped.

Kimara laughed too.

"I can only imagine."

"Movie theater or night at home watching movies?" Brody asked.

"Night at home watching movies. I don't mind an occasional movie out now and then, but I love relaxing at home in my most comfortable worn out shorts and t-shirt in front of a table full of snacks and watching one movie after the other. What about you?" she asked.

"Hands down movies at home beat out anything else. I know people rush out to see movies when they first come out, but these days, if you wait a month or two, the movie is out on several digital platforms and I prefer the relaxation of being at home, especially when I need to wind down from a busy day. Cat or dog?" he asked.

"Both!" Kimara exclaimed a little louder than she'd planned.

"Wow – I see something really excites you."

"I love animals. When I was little, I thought I'd grow up and raise animals on my own farm. Cats and dogs would have been a big part of that. I have a dog and a cat at home and they play like brother and sister. You?"

"I love animals, but if I had to choose, I'd say dog. Journee always points to every dog we see and screams, 'puppy'. I'm thinking of getting her one because I want her to learn to love animals."

"How about, play sports or watch sports?" Kimara asked.

"Here is where I take my cue from your last response by saying both. I enjoy playing a good game of football or basketball with friends and I still believe the greatest pastime is watching sports on Sunday afternoons. You?" he asked.

"I enjoy watching them, especially football. I'm too much of a girl to play sports. I'm not a fan of running or throwing a ball of any kind, but I enjoy watching those who do. I love the WNBA as much as I love watching NBA games."

"Okay, summer or winter?" Brody asked.

"Winter."

"Really? Most people say summer."

"I don't live in a wintery state, but I love the snow, I always have," she said.

"As for me, I love summer. The says seem longer and being on this island in this hot weather, I'm loving everything about it."

"Another for you. Talk or text?" Kimara asked.

"That's the easiest one yet. Definitely talk. I know the world hides from having conversations with each other by texting, but I still prefer the good old talking on the phone. I may text a quick, short note, but if I'm having an extended conversation, it definitely has to be by telephone."

"That's another thing we have in common. I once met a guy in person and we took a little time to know a little about each other and the conversation went well. We exchanged numbers and all he wanted to do was text after that. You can learn more and not assume anything when you talk to people."

"I agree. We could do this all day and I would never tire of getting to know everything about you. I hope that's not too much?" Brody asked.

What he was finding was the more he spent time with and talked to Kimara, he wanted to know even more. He felt a connection to her that he can't remember ever having with another woman before and he liked it. He also really liked her.

"I agree."

They turned when they heard others coming toward them.

"Looks like we're being invaded. To be continued later?" he asked.

Kimara smiled. "I hope so," she said.

"Hey, you two. We're about to head back to the island to get ready for some golf. You game?" Jessica asked.

"Yes!" they said in unison.

"Wow, I see your great minds think alike. You make the cutest couple," Jessica said before turning around.

"I think she's right," Brody said.

Kimara nodded her head, afraid to admit that she was enjoying Brody and hadn't expected the good vibes that flowed between them. Unafraid, she was going to go with the flow.

Chapter 9

Dancing. Whoever came up with dancing deserves a prize, Brody thought to himself. In his arms, he held the most beautiful woman in the world. Kimara had amazed him since the moment he saw her and she continued to do so and now holding her as they danced to the Reggae sounds of Bob Marley he didn't feel the presence of anyone else in the room, but her.

After a day of more excursion activities than he would usually do in an entire year, they agreed to meet for dinner and dancing. He was happy to know that with their vacation package, they were able to go from one resort to the other and decided to venture out and check out dinner at another resort. To their delight, the on-sight night club was playing Reggae music all night and so they leaped at the opportunity to join in. That type of music, it seems, was another thing they had in common.

As the music played and they swayed, Brody held Kimara as close to him as he could while trying to remember a time in his recent past that he'd been this comfortable and relaxed with a woman. He was no angel when it came to hooking up with the opposite sex, but Kimara was different. He felt more like himself than ever before.

Moving his hands in a circular motion across her back, he leaned down to her ear which was a whisper away from his mouth.

"Thank you for an incredible day and for agreeing to go dancing with me tonight. I've wanted to hold you and dancing is a good way to do that," he said.

Kimara leaned back and smiled.

"I never thought I would meet anyone like you when I decided to take this trip. You have helped make this vacation one of the best of my life," she said.

Kimara held onto Brody a little tighter. Though the room had little light, she could see the whites of his eyes and she couldn't look away. Being drawn to his handsome face was becoming a natural occurrence since they'd met. Brody had an intoxicating impact on her and everything about her was sensitive to his touch and definitely to his gaze. She felt like she was waiting for something but didn't know what.

In his eyes, she saw want, need and desire, exactly what she knew her own eyes were reflecting back to him. Kimara was still perplexed over how she could feel such a strong connection to a man after two days.

"Thank you for sharing your day with me," Brody said and pulled her closer as they swayed.

"I had the best day today from going deep sea diving, to sky diving, to zip lining and then dinner and dancing with the best dance partner a girl could ask for. I swear I don't know how much more perfect this whole day could have been. I did things today that I never would have dreamed of doing. Me, zip lining and enjoying it? Not to mention I thought I had a fear of heights and now I think I've dispelled that notion," Kimara said.

"Well, sweetheart, I have a feeling a lot of firsts have been happening these past two days."

Brody didn't say more and was silent about the fact that he believed he'd fallen in love at first sight for the first time. He didn't want to scare her off. They were like two lovers who had been kindred spirits for a lifetime. They were that perfect together and when they talked, he felt like he could tell her everything about him and she'd always give him her undivided attention.

Over dinner, they shared more about each other and he learned that she loved doing consulting work and realized they had someone in common. One of the firms Kimara did consulting work for was owned by one of his clients who turned out to be a good friend named Marjorie.

They had fun talking about their work and families. He learned that Kimara had a sister that she was as close to as he was to his twin, Brynne. Kimara loved hearing all of the twin stories he loved sharing with her.

He and Brynne had always been two peas in a pod and where most boy and girl twins were fraternal, they were identical. He'd joked that if he would let his hair grow out and dye it, they would look like twin girls instead of twin brother and sister. He did notice what they both stayed away from was diving deeper into what had happened and was happening in their lives on a personal level. They did discuss that neither was married or seriously involved, but they never talked about why or what they had gone through that drew them to the island. He wasn't ready to share yet and it seemed Kimara wasn't either. He was okay with that because he didn't want his reason to bring down their time together. The trip was to be all about fun.

Perhaps like him, Kimara was trying to live in the moment they were in without getting too serious. He was okay with that. Eventually, they would return to their lives and put their time on the island behind them. For the moment, they were being what they each needed.

"It's getting late and I know your feet are dying for a soak in the tub. Are you ready to head back? Looks like it's another late night for us." They had been out late the night before when they'd first met. To him, the day still wasn't long enough.

"I don't know what possessed me to wear those heels. I wear them often at home and have never had a problem before. Yes, I'm ready."

Brody took her hand as they walked as he did the night before. Tonight, there was something different about the feel.

Kimara was sad that they had reached her villa sooner than she wanted. They were at a night spot that was closer to her end of the resort so a few minutes of walking and they had arrived.

Brody turned to her as they reached her gate.

"I hope I'm not taking up all of your time. I'm sure you came for just as much relaxation as you did for outside activities."

"No, not at all. I'm having a great time, the best time," Kimara said.

"No more than I am with you. These have been the best two days that I've spent in a long time without worrying about work or what's happening at home. I guess I'm doing what a place like this was created for which is to learn how to let go, relax and enjoy the moment," Brody said.

"I think we're both doing that. You, Brody, are a breath of fresh air. I'm glad we met."

When he didn't respond, Kimara didn't know what to make of his silence. Perhaps she had said too much.

Brody moved closer to Kimara in an attempt to make sure that even with the darkness of the night sky, she would be able to not only hear, but see his sincerity.

"We've spent two nights and a full day getting to know each other and I very much like what I know about you. I don't want anything between us to be awkward, but all day, I've been wondering what it would be like to kiss you, but I've held back because I'm not sure if that would offend you or not. I'm hoping it won't because if I'm correct, I think you feel something happening between us just as I do," he said.

Brody wanted to be sincere and wanted her to know that he didn't want to play around what was growing between them. The sexual chemistry was off the chains, more of a connection than he has ever felt for another woman after knowing her for only a day. Kimara was special and with the time they had left on the island, he wanted to enjoy even more of her if she were open to it.

Kimara blinked as she looked into Brody's eyes. They were standing so close together that even at night, she could see the twinkle in his light brown eyes and her body reacted to the desire she saw in them.

"I do, but what do we do about that. I'm leaving in a few days and the time here will be over."

"What about just focusing on the time we have left. I don't know about you, but I'd like to explore what those few days could mean. I don't want to focus too much on that tonight because we've both had a few drinks, though we're not drunk. I want us to think about exploring a little more, but when we've had time to think about it."

Kimara giggled. She had been thinking the same thing. She'd had two drinks with dinner and dancing, which was two more than she usually had. That wasn't enough to cloud her judgement, but Brody was right.

"I was thinking about that because if I can be really honest here, I was thinking about you and those lips of yours and then that led to thoughts of feeling those same lips all over me and I wasn't sure if it was me or the alcohol thinking," Kimara confessed.

Brody smiled.

"I like you Kimara. I like you a lot and I've been fighting with myself to keep a respectful distance when what I really want to do is hold you in my arms and kiss you until I feel the need to breathe. Every time I look at you or hold hands with you, my desire to kiss you takes over and then I push it back because I don't want you to think that I came on the island and have been spending time with you for any reason other than I like you. I also want to be open and honest with you. It's been a while since I've wanted a woman as much as I want you. I think we both could use a good night's sleep and we can discuss anything more tomorrow. Like you said, you have a few more days and so do I. There is no reason to rush here. I would like to kiss you goodnight," he said and waited.

"I'd like that, too," Kimara said. The anticipation of the kiss was driving her mad. Every time they were together, she wondered if they would ever take that first step and share a kiss. She didn't have to wait much longer as she watched with baited breath as Brody lowered his head to hers. She sucked in a breath just as his mouth came down on hers softly. The touch of his lips to hers sent spirals of unbridled lust and passion through her body making her sex jumped like never before. The kiss that started out slow and massaging was now turning into a power-packed wallop, pretty much blowing her mind.

In her head, she could hear screams of hunger coming from her as he deepened the kiss and merged his tongue with hers where they dueled in connected madness.

All of her senses were heightened by the soft, yet powerful feel of his tongue as he mated with her, eliciting visuals of what it would be like to be made love to by him.

Brody was tossed back and forth by the mesmerizing impact of finally tasting Kimara's lips. He couldn't seem to get enough as he pulled her closer to him, knowing and not caring that she would feel his hard as steel desire for her, intimately wedged between them. He didn't want to be shy about his want for her.

He suckled at her delectable lips again and again like a desperate man who needed the taste of her to survive. He had planned on kissing her lightly and releasing her even though he knew a cold shower would be in his immediate future.

What blew him away was how passionately she joined him in the kiss. He thought he was giving her something to remember about their night, yet instead, she was giving him a kiss that would make him yearn for more and more every time he saw her.

Finally, pulling away after one last taste of her lips, Brody stood to his full height, keeping his eyes on her.

"Wow!" he exclaimed. "I better go before we end up inside together," he said.

"This kiss had more than just an imprint on my lips," Kimara admitted.

"Mine, too. I don't want there to be any doubt that I want you, but tonight, I'm going to call it a night after I make sure you're inside safely. Join me for breakfast in the morning?" he asked.

"Nothing could keep me from it. Thank you for a wonderful day."

"Likewise. Go ahead and go in before I change my mind about leaving," he joked.

Kimara smiled and turned toward the door. She turned briefly and waved at Brody as her heart beat erratically in her chest.

"Tomorrow," she said.

"Tomorrow," Brody replied and watched until the light inside of her villa came on. He then turned around, as he had the night before and headed to his own room. He hoped the next night, they would be going inside together.

Chapter 10

"Kimmy! I've been waiting to hear from you. If it wasn't for the texts you sent to let us know you were doing okay, I would have been blowing up your phone. Are you enjoying yourself?" Casey asked.

Where Kimara thought she would have felt bad about not calling her mother and sister each day, she couldn't help but smile at what and who had held her attention. In the light of day after a night out with Brody, she woke up smiling about more time with him. She was surprised that she was finally able to fall asleep after the intoxicating kiss they'd shared the night before. She woke up ready for more kissing just like that.

"I'm having the time of my life. I've been parasailing, deep-sea diving, zip-lining, hiking and so much more. The night life here is the best and the food makes me want to be fine with sitting around and getting fat because it tastes that good."

"Wow, listen to the sound of your voice. You are having a good time, aren't you? Here I was thinking we would hear that you've been spending all of your time with your face in a book not venturing out at all."

"Sis, I didn't come here to sit around and I told you that," she said excitedly.

Kimara tried, but couldn't stifle a huge, loud yawn that escaped her lips.

"Wait, what was that? Are you still in bed? What else have you been doing where you're sleeping this late on vacation? Is it a man? Tell me so that I can be jealous!" Casey shouted into the phone.

"After a fun day of excursions, I went to dinner and dancing into the wee hours last night and yes, I'm just getting up and about to head out for the breakfast buffet. You're calling mighty early," she said.

"I know, but I thought you would have called yesterday, but now I guess I understand why you didn't. I see you ignored my comment about a man, so what gives? Met any sexy island men yet? Please tell me yes!"

Kimara shook her head. The moment Casey mentioned man, her body tingled all over with thoughts of Brody and all of that sexiness walking back down the beach last night. She'd watched him from her window as he strolled away and she wanted to shout out for him to come in and join her for more than just kissing, but he was right, they needed to take a little time and think about what more time together would mean. Was she ready to take that step with any man? She hadn't since Ellis, but there was something so seductive and uninhibited about Brody that made her anxious to get closer to him.

First, she needed to get her sister off of her back. They always talked about everything, so there was no need to try and lie her way out of her time on the island.

"Yes, I met a man and no, he's not an islander. He's here on vacation like I am."

"Yes!" Casey screamed.

Kimara had to hold her cell phone away from her face when Casey screamed.

"Really Casey? Is it that serious?" she asked and laughed.

"Are you serious? This is very serious because it's you. In five years, I have never heard you entertain a conversation about a man and after a few days on an island, you boldly tell me you've met one. So, what have the two of you been doing and will I need to smoke a cigarette after this conversation?" Casey joked.

"Funny, sis. So far, we've done excursions together, talked and danced and just having a good time. He's tall, handsome and gorgeous. He actually defies the word handsome. This brother is fine, girl!" Kimara boasted.

"Yes! That's what I'm talking about. Get you some, sis and in fact, get you a lot. Have you done it yet? Now, before you go all postal on me, sorry, but not sorry for digging into your business. I'm just excited to hear you talking about a man."

"You act like I've been living in a convent or something. I know a good-looking man when I see one and Brody is one."

"Ah, his name is Brody and he's fine. Nice. Did he do *IT* for you? You know what I'm talking about," Casey said.

"We haven't done *THAT*, or at least not yet. I think we will or I hope we will. I mean, I don't know," Kimara stammered.

"Uh, oh, you're stuttering. This guy must be something. I'm happy to hear you're having a good time. Remember the condoms I packed for you. Don't be shy about using every single one of them. It's okay to be single, free and sexual.

Nothing says you have to locked down and committed before getting you some nasty, nasty! I say get it and get it a lot."

Kimara had to hold her hand over her mouth to hide the cough that escaped her throat. She loved her sister, but sometimes her way of pushing the envelope and saying what's on her mind could be a little too much to deal with.

"You know I may not be all sex-crazed like my sister, but I know what to do and how to do it," she said.

"Are you sure? I'm just saying, it's been a long while for you unless you've been keeping secrets from me," Casey insinuated.

Kimara exhaled.

"I'm not keeping any secrets from you. You know Ellis has been my one and only and he still is. I do like Brody and the way he kissed me last night left me with all kinds of feelings and desires stirring up that had been dormant for a long time. I'm meeting him for breakfast if you ever let me off the phone to get dressed."

"Well, don't let me be the hold up. Maybe I'll get to meet this Brody one day if this island thing becomes more than just a fling," Casey added.

"No. What happens on this island will stay on this island. I'm not looking for more than enjoying myself while I'm here."

"Is he just someone to get some from and that's it?"

Kimara jumped in immediately to defend her words and Brody.

"No, not at all. He is the complete opposite of someone like that. I can't understand why a man as successful and handsome as Brody is would still be single, but he is. He said he doesn't have a wife or girlfriend at home, but he does have a young daughter."

"So, that means he is probably divorced or just some woman's baby-daddy. Nothing wrong with that. You said he's successful. What does he do?"

"He's vice president at a bank and before you ask, I have no idea which one. I don't even know what state he lives in. We haven't share everything. It's only been two days. He really is an incredible man and not just sexy. There is more to him, but we are on this island and whatever happens is short term. When I leave here, I'm leaving what happens right here on this island. If nothing else, Brody has reminded me of how desirable and sexy I am and how much I have been missing out on by shutting myself off from being involved with someone. I won't do that again. For now, I'm enjoying getting to know him and we'll see what the possibilities are for the time I have remaining on the island. Now, I need to get moving before the breakfast buffet is over and Brody thinks I'm not coming."

"Okay, Kimmy. I'm glad you're having a good time and shout out to this guy for bringing out the freak in you again!" Casey said while laughing out loud.

"Whatever. Love you, sis."

Kimara hung up and rushed to get dressed. The last thing she wanted was for Brody to think she wasn't coming.

**

"I'm only calling to check on how Journee is doing. Mom and Pop, I'm sure have their hands full with her," Brody said as he walked onto the outside platform where the buffet breakfast was being served. He'd gotten up later than he'd planned after tossing and turning most of the night with thoughts of Kimara invading his mind. He ended up having to take two cold showers in order to get his body to calm down after the kiss they shared. He was indeed enthralled by her and the feel of her lips on his was scrumptious. He couldn't wait to experience those lips again.

"Did you hear me?" Brynne inquired.

"What? I didn't hear you say anything. What did I miss?" he said, clearly not focused on the conversation.

"What's distracting you?" Brynne asked.

"I'm not distracted."

"Yes, you are and I want to know what or who has you unfocused."

"Are you going to tell me what you said or not? I'm about to eat breakfast," he said.

"I said, Journee is doing good and she is spending the night with us tonight. The boys miss her and she wanted to hang with me tonight."

Brody looked up just as he sat down at a table before checking out the buffet. When he first arrived, he looked around for Kimara, but didn't see her. She must have overslept like he had. He was about to turn around, when something on the side caught his attention. Kimara was walking out and from what he could see, she was a vision of beauty, walking, but floating on air at the same time. She was wearing a thin, short strappy dress that moved with her gorgeous hips as she walked. No matter how many times he saw her, he would never be able to get over how extraordinarily beautiful she was.

"Kimara, over here!" he shouted and waved to her.

"Kimara? Who is Kimara," Brynne asked.

Brody was glad he didn't have time to explain.

"She's a friend and I have to go. Kiss Journee for me. I'll

call later so that I can talk to her before she goes to bed. Love you, Brynne."

"But...."

Brody hung up even though he could hear the wheels in Brynne's head turning when she heard him call out for Kimara. That would be a conversation for another time. Right now, he had a gorgeous woman walking his way and he wanted to give her all of his attention.

"Good morning, beautiful," Brody said the minute Kimara joined him at the table.

"Yes, it is and good morning to you."

"I was just about to get something to eat from the buffet. I see we're both getting a late start today," he said.

"I was planning to be up earlier, but I had a late night," Kimara smiled.

"As did I. My mind couldn't rest and focus on sleep after that kiss last night."

"So, it wasn't just me," she said, happy to hear that she wasn't the only one struggling with the fact that she didn't want the night to end with her going to bed alone.

"Not at all. Perhaps, tonight, we can figure out a way that we can equally get some sleep."

Brody made sure to speak and gaze deeply into her eyes. In the light of day with a clear mind and focus, he wanted to be sure he was being plain and transparent about how his desire for her couldn't lead to another night of him leaving her at her villa while he went back to his. If he had any say, they would be spending the night together tonight.

"What did you have in mind?" Kimara asked, open and ready for what the night could bring.

"What do you say to me cooking dinner for you tonight in

my villa? That is, if you're comfortable with that," Brody suggested.

"You cook?" she asked, surprised.

"I do. You mentioned you love Italian and seafood. I would love to spend time with you tonight either in your place or mine. I'll let you choose which works best for you if you're open to that," he said, leaving the ball fully in her court. There was no need to have an in-depth discussion about what the evening together would mean. They were two adults and the sexual vibe between them was off the scales. He was more than ready to indulge if she was.

Kimara never thought for once to hesitate. She knew what she wanted even if she was as nervous as nervous could be.

"I would love that and I don't mind coming to your villa if that's okay with you. Do you have what you would need to actually cook a meal or would it be easier to order something to be delivered to the room?" she asked.

"I can get what I need and I would prefer to dazzle you with my cooking abilities, among other things. Are you ready for that?" he asked, making sure she understood the double-entendre associated with his response.

"If I'm not, I plan to be. We have a few days left and I don't want to waste them," she said.

Brody picked up her hand and kissed the back of it, with his eyes locked on hers.

"Neither do I. Let's get breakfast and then I'll leave you to enjoy your day however you like while I work on preparing for the perfect evening. Dinner around seven?" he asked.

"Seven sounds great," Kimara replied.

As Brody stood and took her hand, they walked to the breakfast buffet. She hoped he couldn't tell that she was walking on shaky legs. She was excited and nervous about the night ahead of her because as much as he wanted her, she wanted him, too.

Chapter 11

Brody stirred the penne pasta just as it began to boil. He eyed the marinara sauce as it simmered slowly with seasonings that cast a rich aroma throughout the villa. The garlic and wine sautéed shrimp that was already done was resting in a bowl waiting to be added to the sauce. Opening the oven door, he checked on the three cake pans that would make up his almost famous triple chocolate layered cake, a recipe his mother passed to him and his sister that she'd gotten from her grandmother years ago.

Brody smile, happy that he was able to get all of the items for the dinner he was cooking for Kimara with the help of the resort concierge, a man who took his job knowing the ins and outs of the island serious.

He was ecstatic that Kimara accepted his invitation to dinner and to exploring an intimate evening with him if that was how the night turned out. He wasn't placing any pressure on her, but he couldn't deny the immediate attraction he felt toward her the moment he saw her and with the time they'd been spending together, he couldn't help the desirous whoosh that flowed through his body every time he laid eyes on her.

Kimara was the most beautiful woman he'd ever met, inside and out. Never in his wildest dreams did he think he'd take a vacation and come across a woman he'd want to spend all of his time with.

The night before, they talked briefly about making the most of their time on the island without any pressure and earlier in the day, they were both clear that they wanted to explore the vibe that was growing between them.

While they ate breakfast, they talked about what spending the evening together would mean and he wanted her to know that he wasn't holding her to any expectations beyond what they were sharing on the island. He was leaving what could happen between them up to her. Neither knew what life after the island would be like for them, so they decided to not think beyond it and just enjoy the moment.

As he opened the refrigerator door, he looked inside at all of the ingredients for the making of the salad he still needed to pull together. The bottle of wine sat chilling at the end of the white and gray marble counter while soft music played in the background from his phone that he'd synced with the sound system in the villa. He loved that it played throughout in every room.

Reaching to grab what he needed to start on the salad, Brody heard a soft knock on the door. Kimara was early and he smiled in anticipation of seeing her again. Though they had agreed to leave what happened on the island, on the island, he had a feeling that once he got a taste of her, that would be hard to do. There was something special about Kimara. For now, he would honor their agreement and enjoy the moment and the time they had left to spend together.

Rushing to the door, he swung it opened and for an instant his heart stopped beating. Before him, Kimara stood glowing and almost exotic like someone out of a romantic dream. He knew his mouth hung open as he looked her over from head to toe, stopping to admire the soft pink, flowing dress with thin straps. The smile that greeted him gave him a sense of peace that wove throughout his body. He immediately knew that the woman who stood before him would not be an island fling he would be able to forget about. Everything about her was already seared as a permanent imprint in his head and if he were honest with himself, in his heart.

"Well, hello there," Brody said, finally able to speak.

"Hi. I'm hope I'm not too early," Kimara said walking into the room when Brody moved to the side.

"You being too early would never happen. You look incredible," he said.

"Thank you. You know, you are very complimentary and not many men these days do that anymore. It's refreshing to have met a man who makes a woman feel as special as you have made me feel since the moment we met."

Kimara turned and faced him after he closed and double locked the door behind them.

"I believe a woman should be complimented every time a man opens his mouth. Maybe then, for those who often say something stupid, they will be detoured to something flattering instead. Besides, it's easy when it comes to you."

"A girl could get used to being around you with all of this smooth talking and just so you know, I love it," Kimara said, smiling.

"Well, in that case, beautiful, be prepared to be wowed

over the next couple of days because I have an unlimited library of words to make you swoon. Now, how about you come in and I'll fix you a glass of wine."

Kimara took the hand that Brody extended to her and like the first night when their hands touched while walking on the beach, she felt an electric current that caressed her body like a hot summer night cradled by a lover. It was a zap of familiarity that was existing between them that neither of them could deny.

"Did you feel that?" she said.

Kimara didn't want to be the only one who felt it just in case it wasn't real.

Brody turned to her.

"You mean like the jolt the other night when we held hands walking on the beach? Yeah, I felt it then and I feel it now. I felt it last night when we kissed. I feel it every time I'm near you. I won't scare you away by telling you the affect touching you keeps having on my entire body," Brody said as his voice dropped to a deep, seductive tone. When they were together, the vibe in the air exuded all kinds of sexiness.

"Trust me, it's not a feeling that only you are experiencing. I could really use that glass of wine," Kimara said smiling while holding on to his hand a little tighter.

Brody could see Kimara looked flushed. There was more happening between the two of them than either of them could fathom, nor could they resist it.

"That's good to know because that means the way I feel connected to you isn't something I'm dreaming up. Have a seat at the counter and I'll get some glasses," he said.

Brody could use a bit of a break himself. He felt intoxicated every time Kimara was around and just now, he knew if he hadn't made an excuse to give them some breathing room, he would have picked her up and carried her straight to the bedroom.

"Your villa is beautiful. It's similar to mine, but the décor here is manlier while mine is made for a woman. Lots of light, bright colors a lady would love. The hues in shades of brown in here fit you."

"Yeah, I like it. I hear that's why they ask a lot of questions when you book your trip, so that they can make sure your stay is as comfortable as possible."

"Something smells wonderful. What are you cooking?" Kimara asked.

Ethan poured them each a glass of white wine and quickly checked on the food.

"Well, you told me you liked Italian food, so I whipped up a little something. There is marinara sauce with garlic sautéed shrimp and chicken over penne pasta. I'm steaming some asparagus and I have the mixings for a salad in the refrigerator that I still need to make and to top off the evening, I'm making my mother's recipe for a triple chocolate layered cake."

"Wow! That is amazing. Everything sounds and smells so good. Where did you learn to cook?"

"My mother taught me as I was growing up. She said just in case I never married, she didn't want me showing up at her house for dinner every night. I've been cooking since my teenage years and yes, I enjoy cooking very much," Brody acknowledged.

"I love to cook also."

"What's your specialty?"

"I enjoy cooking seafood, using various sauces and

seasonings to change up the flavor. Is there anything I can help with? I see you moving from pot to pot and I feel like I should be doing something."

Brody moved about taking the now done cake out of the oven to cool until it was time to add frosting.

"I haven't made the salad yet. All of the ingredients are in the fridge if you want to start that."

Kimara got up, washed her hands and began pulling out what she needed.

"You were able to get all of my favorite makings for a salad. Where did you find all of this food?" Kimara asked.

"From the best concierge on the island. I gave him a list and he hooked me up with everything I needed. Dinner is actually just about ready. I hope you're hungry because there's a lot of food."

Brody was proud of himself. He was on a date that didn't feel as casual as his usual dates with women. That's how he knew Kimara was different and he hoped he was making her feel special.

He watched as she laid everything out on the counter before grabbing a bowl he had already set out for her to wash and strain. When she looked over at him and their eyes met, Brody found himself lost in the deep, dark pools. Her beauty was becoming intoxicating and he wanted her with a fierceness that he forgot he could possess. Women had been coming and going over the past few years, but Kimara was what he would call long-term potential. He wanted more than just the physical with her. He hadn't been this comfortable around a woman since....

He ended the thought of comparing Kimara to anything and anyone. He had fallen for her and there was no turning back.

"No cucumbers," Kimara said, stunned and wondering if that was a coincidence or something else.

"No cucumbers," Brody replied as he turned the fire off under all of the remaining pots.

"How did you know I don't care for cucumbers or was that just a fluke?" she asked.

Brody smile. "No fluke involved here. I noticed when you made salads from the buffet each time we ate and you skipped over the cucumbers. I assumed they weren't your cup of tea."

"Very observant," she said and turned toward the sink to begin rinsing everything off.

"It's easy to observe when my eyes land on everything about you. I hope that doesn't make you uncomfortable."

"Far from it. I've never been this comfortable around a man after knowing him a few short days. I like how it feels."

Brody tried to resist, but no longer could. They had been dancing around and flirting with each other from the moment they met. Now having her here and as comfortable with him as he was with her, was a sign that the fact that he couldn't stop thinking about her even when they were apart was also not a fluke. It was destiny.

Walking over to her, Brody stood behind her, placing his hands on the counter on either side of her. Moving close to her neck, he heard her breath catch as he leaned in, placing a soft kiss on the side of her neck, which was exposed with her hair pulled high on her head.

"What about that? How does that feel?" he asked and then kissed her neck again, just as softly as he had the first time. This time he felt her shiver and the feeling vibrated through him.

"That feels incredible. You are incredible," Kimara said and turned around slowly until they were face to face. She looked up into Brody's eyes and the desire in them warmed her from the inside out as heat rushed through her. She held her breath as he moved closer to her face until there was barely any room between them, something she welcomed. In her head she was screaming for him to kiss her, to pull her into his arms and deal with the ache that was pulsating between her legs.

"You are beautiful inside and out, sexy and absolutely astonishing. Any man would be lucky to hear those words come from your mouth. I'm happy knowing what's happening between us is mutual."

"It's very mutual if what I'm reading on your face is the same as what I know is on my mind," Kimara said.

"What's going on in that pretty mind of yours?" Brody said.

Kimara was nervous and hoped it didn't show. She was never one to be open about her wants and desires, but everything about Brody warmed her and gave her a comfortable feeling that she could share anything with him and it would be okay. Could she do it? Could she say out loud how much she wanted him? What would it mean? An island fling? Is that all she wanted from him? They had lives to go back to and she didn't want to invade that or ask for more than what he was probably offering. She had no doubt he didn't come on vacation in search of a long-term relationship and neither did she. Could she seek out the desires that flowed through her and walk away in a few days? Men did it all the time, but women operated more on feelings and were more vested when it came to relationships of any kind, especially sexual ones.

"I.....," was all she could get out.

Brody saw her shyness and sensed she wasn't used to being put on the spot to talk openly about what she wanted. He didn't want her moving from comfortable to an uncomfortable place with him.

"How about I confirm for you what you see in my eyes?" When Kimara nodded, he smiled. "What you see is a man who desires you as much as he desires to take his next breath. From the very moment I saw you, I've wanted you, but I do admit, it has turned into more than that. What we have is right now. What we have is our time on this island and if I can spend it making love to you, I would be a man more than grateful that you desired the same. In a few days, we'll go back to our lives, but right now, I want you and I'm hoping that the feeling is mutual.

Dipping his head down, Brody placed a soft opened mouth kiss on Kimara's lips, not taking his eyes from her face as she closed her eyes and enjoyed their connection. He was about to move back when he felt Kimara's soft hands reach out to hold on to his shirt, keeping him in place. That invitation was all he needed as he kissed her again, this time deeply, relishing in the seductive way she returned the kiss adding an ardent fervor that told him she was just as ready for him as he was for her.

Brody gripped the marble counter top, trying his best not to grab hold of Kimara's hips, afraid his uncontrollable lust for her would cause him to grip her too tight. His body was on fire and the way she was kissing him back threw his want to another level that wasn't even measurable. Through the kiss, he could hear a soft mewling sound coming from her lips and that fueled him even more.

"More," Kimara said when he pulled away so that they could breathe, noticing her breaths were as deep as his.

If nothing else, Brody always obliged a woman in his arms. Bringing her closer, he reached up and placed his hand on the back of her head while the other rested on her hip as he took the kiss from exotic to wild in mere seconds. He felt her arms circle his waist as their heads moved around trying to get closer and closer to each other. All of the passion he had been holding in was being poured into the kiss and he wasn't the only one who had been holding it back. Kimara was kissing him like a woman who was having the last kiss she would ever share with a man. He was so turned on, he couldn't seem to get enough of her lips. Once again, he pulled back and kept his eyes on hers. What they were experiencing was more than a casual connection. He now knew it was much deeper than that. He had just experienced the kiss of a lifetime and from the way Kimara was looking back at him, she was experiencing it, too.

After placing one last, quick kiss on her lips, Brody leaned his forehead against hers while he willed his body to calm down. He was on fire!

"You're killing me, Kimara," he said, trying to regain some composure. Leaning back, he waited for Kimara to tell him that it was time for dinner or that the kissing was enough – anything to help him channel a less aroused Brody. He watched as a sexy grinned covered Kimara's face right before she parted her lips to speak, lips he was already feigning to kiss again.

"If we don't stop right now, dinner is going to be freezing

cold by the time we get to it because the only thought on my mind right now is where the closest bed is," she said nervously. Surprising herself, she knew that she had never been this brazen before, but being with Brody felt natural and she felt like a superwoman. She had asked for more during the kissing, but that wasn't enough and she'd just put it out there, hoping Brody didn't see her as being too forward.

Looking from his eyes to those sexy lips that were doing amazing things to every part of her body, she kept her eyes on him as he leaned in close to her ear.

"I'm ready for you and there is a bed with our names on it in the next room," he said. "Shall we?" he added.

Kimara shivered as Brody's deep baritone voice spoke to her and setting off embers that could only be doused once they were naked. Her heart beat wildly in her chest at the thought of what being ready for her meant. Already, with them standing as close as they are, she could feel his hardness pressed up against her.

Dinner was the furthest thing from her mind and from the way he felt long and hard against her, they were on the same page.

"Yes," she said without hesitating.

Brody kissed her again.

"I see a microwave that we can use to heat the food up later. Right now, I have another hunger that needs you pretty badly."

Kimara could relate.

"I'm starving and it's not about food. I'm starving for you and me, naked so that this sensual ache I feel every time I'm around you can settle down," she said and knew that Brody could read the level of pleading she was conveying not just with her words, but with her eyes.

Brody growled knowing they were on the same page and there was no doubt about what was coming next.

"Are you sure? In a few days we go back to our lives. I need to know you're okay with that," he said.

"I know and I was thinking the same thing. I didn't come here for a fling of any kind, but you are too tempting to let these last few days go by without living the fantasy of being with you. I'm sure if you are," Kimara said and meant it.

Brody looked down at what stood ready between them and laughed.

"I think we both see my confirmation of being sure."

Kimara didn't answer because she had felt it and having him pressed hard against her fueled the fire of desire for him even more. She was ready. Moving out of his arms, she turned and walked toward the bedroom. No more talking, she thought. There was no turning back and she didn't want to. She only wanted him.

"I'll be waiting while you cover the food," she said before winking at him from the doorway. Before going inside, she took being brazen to another level when she reached for the sleeves of her dress and pulled them down until the dress fell to the floor at her feet, leaving her standing before him in a strapless black bra and a barely-there black thong with a thin strap that was lost between the round globes of her behind. She looked over her shoulder as Brody's eyes went up and down her body, paying close attention to her plump, toned behind. She'd have to give her personal trainer an extra tip at her next session.

Throwing more caution to the wind, she raised the

temperature in the room a little more when she did a little wiggle from side to side like a model on a runway and then turned all the way around slowly, giving him his fill of her before walking into the room out of his view.

"Damn!" was all Brody could think to say as heat that burned like fire shot to every region of his body. Kimara was some woman, he thought and rushed to make sure all of the pots were off, food was covered and placed the salad fixings that Kimara never got to back in the refrigerator. Turning the lights in the main room down low and increasing the volume of the music playing soft jazz throughout the villa, he headed toward the bedroom and the purpose for his body being harder than he ever remembered being before.

Chapter 12

Kimara may not have shown her nervousness in front of Brody, but now as she stood in the middle of the bedroom, she shivered from anticipation of what she knew was going to be a sensual night. She surprised herself by literally dropping her dress and enticing him to join her in the bedroom while donning a bra, panties and stiletto heels. Everything about Brody screamed hot, steamy sex and if her body was an example of being hot like fire, she was more than ready to experience everything she knew he would bring to the bed.

She thought back to the many conversations she and her sister joked about her enjoying herself with a man while on the island, yet she never thought she'd actually do it. It's completely out of character for her to be this excited about being with any man considering how long it had been and how complacent she had become not being intimately involved with anyone, but her body and her mind were vested in being with Brody. There is no way she'd be able to walk away from the deep-seated want overpowering her. The minute she saw him standing in the lobby of the resort, she knew that she would end up exactly where she was if they had a chance to connect and boy did they ever.

Getting a look around the room, she was able to see the difference in their two villas, but one thing was a constant and that was the large bed that sat in the middle of the room. Staring at it, the moment became real. For the first time in five years, she was going to make love with a man, someone she'd just met, but was drawn to in the most provocative way. Her sister was right, there was nothing wrong with enjoying the moment and she knew that what the night had in store for her, she would never forget. She and Brody were clear that they would eventually go back to their lives after leaving the island and she knew that meant leaving what they shared on the island as well. This was her first fling and perhaps, this was her entrance back into the world after having closed herself off from it for so long.

Kimara sensed before she heard the moment Brody entered the room even with her back to him. She turned and encountered eyes that feasted on her and she wasn't the slightest bit uneasy. As their eyes locked and Brody's heated gaze seared through her, his presence spread across the entire room with an aura that spoke of nothing but a night of pure passion and eager salacity. What caught her attention was where her eyes landed as he stood in the doorway looking at her like she was a precious jewel. As she took in his ever-present masculine stance, her eyes traveled to just below his waist where his manhood pressed against the front of his pants, long, erect and more than ready for a night filled with tantalizing seduction.

As he moved toward her, her heart sped up and her palms felt clammy. She wanted this – she wanted him and thankfully, he didn't make her wait. She shivered the moment his hands caressed her bare exposed arms as his eyes never left hers.

"You know, I couldn't focus on how to cover the food for later after you dropped that dress. I knew you were beautiful and would be under those sexy dresses you like to wear, but you, this, I am losing my mind over all that is you. Are you sure about this?" he asked.

Kimara smiled. "You keep asking like my answer is going to change – it's not."

"I want to be sure. Like you, I've never done this before, gone off on an island and had a fling. I know how much I want you."

"I want you, too. I knew it from that first day."

"I'm glad we're here," Brody said as he continued to peruse her body with his eyes.

There was something Kimara needed Brody to know even though she already stood before him practically naked.

"Did I forget to mention that it's been quite a long time for me and by a long time, I mean around five years," Kimara admitted. She wasn't saying it to ruin the moment, but she didn't want him to take her nervousness for doubt about being with him.

"I assume you had a reason for doing so and thank you for sharing that with me. I'll make sure I'm gentle with you."

"Not too gentle though, right?" she asked. If she was going to experience him, she wanted to full experience.

"Anything you want as long as I can get you naked," Brody said. "First, I need a taste of your lips again. You're so soft and inviting and kissing you has already become addictive for me."

Not giving Kimara a chance to speak, Brody did just that. He kissed her and went straight from zero to sixty with the level of intensity off the charts. As they kissed, he reached for the snap on his jeans and used his legs to slide them down and off. Stepping back, he pulled the shirt up and off, standing before her in navy boxer briefs.

Kimara looked down and couldn't contain her excitement. As large as she imagined he was when they stood in the kitchen, it didn't compare to the sheer magnitude of the size of him and being able to see the imprint even more. His briefs came nowhere near to containing all of him.

"Oh, my," she said as her pulse quickened.

"I promise we'll fit perfectly," Brody said, picking her up and laying her before him on the bed. Coming down over her, he kissed her passionately, first her lips and then over as much skin as he could reach.

"Yes," Kimara moaned.

Brody kissed her wildly as her body moved around under him. He loved how responsive she was to him as he kissed his way down her body. Lifting her slightly, he continued kissing her exposed flesh as he unfastened the snap to her bra. As it fell away, he was thankful that sundown wasn't until close to an hour from now and he could see every delightful part of Kimara's body. Seeing her large breasts calling out to him, he couldn't wait to get a taste. Going right for the pebbled nipple that stood out like a homing beacon, he drew the peak into his mouth, caressing it with the pad of his tongue before adding a little pressure with his teeth. The moment her body jerked and her hips went into a circular swirl, Brody knew he was giving her the pleasure she needed and that she had gone too long without. Tonight, was about her.

After paying homage to the other side, he slid further down until he encountered the thin lace of her thong. Kissing all around her hip, he used his teeth to slide the flimsy material down her legs. Before kissing his way back up, he reached into the table next to the bed and withdrew one of the condoms he'd placed there earlier. Planning to make love to her throughout the night, he wasn't in a rush to do everything he wanted to do to her body the first time. What he needed most was to be inside of her and the look on Kimara's face as she watched him open the packet told him she was thinking the same thing.

Removing his briefs, he slid in between her legs, spreading them wider. Before he had a chance to slide the condom on, he felt Kimara's soft hand caress first the head of him and then slide down, getting a feel for his length and width.

"Never have I seen a man this long, hard and thick. My hand doesn't even go all the way around you. You feel velvety smooth in my hand," she whispered breathlessly.

Loving the way her hand moved over him, Brody leaned down and kissed her with an intoxicating zest as he tried to take his mind temporarily off of the way she stroked him, heightening his desire for her. Without thinking, his hips instinctively moved back and forth, in and out of her grip. The friction was almost too much to bear as he moved out of her reach.

"If I let you continue this, trust me, this would be over quick," he laughed.

Finally covering himself, Brody leaned down until his face was at the center of her. He could see from the look on Kimara's face that she was preparing herself for what was about to come. As much as he wanted to be inside of her, he needed to be sure she was ready for him. As soon as his tongue swiped up the middle of her womanhood, he had no doubt she was ready as his tongue encountered a pool of moisture that had already gathered there. Knowing that she was this ready for him, he kissed and suckled at her center, keeping up with the movement of her hips. Using his fingers, he spread her wetness around and unable to wait anymore, he slid up until they were face to face.

"You are so beautiful," Brody said as he joined their lips while also spreading her legs further while gently sliding into her body. He encountered a tightness and took his time giving her a little more of him each time he moved in and out. When he felt Kimara lock her legs behind his back, he slid out and then entered her as far as he could go.

"Oh!" Kimara moaned.

"Ah, you feel amazing," Brody added and then took them higher.

They moved together as nature expected a man and woman to do since the beginning of time.

"So good," Kimara said as she moved in sync with his strokes.

Brody had set the pace, but Kimara was guiding the intensity. Brody stroked into her over and over again and increased the pace as the powerful moment grabbed a hold of them together. He loved her and responded to the way her body responded to him. They loved over and over as they climbed higher and higher. Before long, as his head dropped to plant kisses along the column of Kimara's neck, he could feel that she was close.

"Don't hold back, baby. Let go and fly into ecstasy and

enjoy every single delightful surge that sears through you," he said.

On his last word, Kimara did just that as her body shattered into a million little pieces. She was moving wildly about under Brody and wasn't sure how he'd been able to stay inside of her. Her moves were uncontrolled as her orgasm reached a fever pitch when wave after delicious wave cascaded over her. She knew Brody was intimately connected to her in one place, but she could feel him everywhere and she never wanted the feeling to stop. She kept up the momentum and as Brody growled in her ear, she knew that he was now flying as high as she was. Gripping him with her body's muscles, they bucked wildly together as he let go with a force that rocked the whole bed. Nothing had prepared her for the full force of making love with a man as virile as Brody. She'd never experienced an orgasm as powerful as the one she'd just had. This, she knew, was exactly what she needed.

As their bodies calmed and their strokes softened, Kimara smiled knowing Brody was worth the wait. It was this kind of love making that she needed from a man and with him being a master at pleasing her, she was already looking forward to more.

**

"This dinner is good. There's so much flavor," Kimara bellowed in between bites.

After making love a second time, they were finally parched and Brody had gone into the kitchen to heat up their food. He'd made her promise to stay in bed and not help him because he wanted to cater to her. She did as he asked and enjoyed the glass of wine he returned to the room with in hand before heating up their food. Now, they sat at the small table in the bedroom as soft music played in the background. Kimara was enjoying a perfect night.

"I'm glad you're like it. You know, you look really cute in my t-shirt," Brody said. So that Kimara wouldn't have to put her clothes back on in order to eat, he'd dug out one of his clean shirts for her to wear while he put on a pair of shorts. The last thing he wanted was for her to go back to being fully clothed. If she was willing, he had plans to find their way back to bed after eating. Making love to her only increased his level of desire for her. He didn't think he would ever tire of making love to her although he knew their time was short. Because of that, he wanted to make the most and best of the time they had left. He didn't want to think about the fact that they were going to have to part ways. Though the concept had always been in the back of his mind, it was now forefront that they were going back to their lives and their time together would be over. He wasn't sure he was ready for that. In a different time and place or if he had met her back in Houston, she would be the woman that he would want for more than a casual relationship. Kimara was already becoming more to him.

"Your t-shirt looks like a dress on me," Kimara laughed. "Well, I can't eat another bite," she added leaning back in her chair.

"You don't want dessert? The cake frosted yet, but there is ice cream in the refrigerator if you want some" Brody asked. After spending three hours in bed, the time was close to eleven and on an island like Turks and Caicos, the night was just picking up.

"I can't eat another thing."

What she didn't want to say is that she was leaving her

appetite for more of him.

"You know, I didn't know if you wanted to go to any of tonight's guest events. My selfish choice would be to keep you naked for the rest of the night, but you're on vacation and I don't want to monopolize your time," Brody explained.

"You're too thoughtful for your own good," she said before standing and walking over to him. Maneuvering herself so that she could straddle his lap, the second she sat down on him, that part him that she had already enjoyed more than once already came out to greet her with an offering of more of what she'd already experienced.

"It's a quality I'm proud of," Brody said, leaning forward and kissing her. "You taste delicious," he added.

"That's good because the only thing I want to do tonight and all night is spend it under, over and around you. There is nothing I want to do more than to continue to feel the way you've been making me feel. Unless you have something you wanted to indulge in tonight, I'm all yours," she explained. Kimara didn't want any gray area surrounding what was a priority for her. Tonight, it was her time with him.

"It seems we are once again on the same page. The only thing I want to indulge in is you and I'm thinking dessert is going to have to wait," he said standing with Kimara in his arms and heading over to the bed. The moment he removed the t-shirt from her body and dropped his shorts, Brody knew that they were in for the night and he was going to make it a memorable one.

Chapter 13

"Brody Grey," Kimara said out loud to no one since she was back in her villa alone. After spending the night with Brody, they'd woken up, had breakfast together, which he'd had delivered to his villa and before returning to her own room, they made love again and did so in the shower where she boldly joined him. Her body shivered as she remembered how he happily let her know that he was overjoyed about her decision. Now, in the privacy of her own space, to her dismay, she was already missing him. How could she feel so connected to a man so quickly? She knew how because Brody was intense, loving and attentive like any woman would love for a man to be. Her biggest problem was the fact that since they met, she had been unable to think about anything else and now that they'd been intimate, she felt like everything about him was blazoned on her.

After making love for a third time the night before, they laid awake and talked. Though they didn't talk about the reason behind why they were both on the island, something she knew must be as major for him as it was for her, they did talk about work and she loved hearing him talk about his daughter. She could tell that he was a doting father, something she loved. She had longed for children, though it didn't happen for her and she wasn't sure it ever would.

Brody was an amazing man who loved spending time with his family, including his twin sister, Brynne. She'd shared with him the closeness she shared with her own sister and how she'd convinced her to take the trip she was currently on. They talked for over an hour before intimacy took over and they made love into the wee hours of the morning. She was tired when they finally got out of bed in the morning, but she would do it all over again, not changing anything.

One thing that stood out from their conversation was the fact that they were both from Houston. She couldn't believe how ironic that was. She'd driven by the bank where he worked many times and they even liked some of the same eateries. They couldn't have come across each other while in Houston because she would have remembered him. Brody had a presence that couldn't be ignored. How could they both be from Houston and not once remember seeing each other. They even had Marjorie in common, someone she did consulting work for. She was a customer of Brody's yet their worlds never crossed. She wanted to know more.

Pulling out her laptop, she was already struggling with whether to invade Brody's life by checking out references to him on the internet. How invasive could it be since she'd shared her body with him. She loved that they were getting to know each other, but something pricked at her that wouldn't go away. There was a familiarity that nagged at her.

Opening up her web browser, she typed in his name. She noticed a few articles about him and his business acumen where he was celebrated for helping to bring major building projects to the Texas area. His expertise in corporate finance bode well for him in his career. What caught her off guard was a reference to Brody and his wife Peyton.

The headline took her breath away. Clicking on the article to bring up the full story, she realized she and Brody shared a past that neither of them knew about. She was stunned to read that Brody, like her, had lost his spouse as a result of a train crash and even more stunning was the fact that it had been the same crash.

Though Ellis had died immediately, Brody's wife Peyton had been kept alive so that their daughter whom she was still pregnant with could have a chance at life. She tried to think back to that time and couldn't remember making the connection that Brody was a part of the group of families that had lost someone. A lot of the families impacted had become close and even attended counseling together in order to deal with their grief. She knew if Brody had been a part of that, she would have remembered.

As she read the story of the love between Brody and Peyton, tears fell down her cheeks. He had refused to do any interviews and never spoke publicly though he did agree to the article that was written about the tragedy and the love he shared with his wife. She could relate to that kind of love because she had shared that with Ellis.

Kimara could understand why Brody didn't want to spend a lot of time focusing on the publicity aspect of the crash since he had a daughter he needed to focus on and it appears from the article that Journee had indeed taken a rough ride into the world, proof that she was meant to survive.

Closing the laptop, she leaned back in the chair and thought back over the conversations they'd shared. None of them involved the fact that his wife and her husband had died. They only shared that they were both single and needed to get away for a much-needed vacation. She understood even more about him, especially about the pain he had to have gone through back then.

Life had been its roughest for her and her trip to the island was so that she could finally come to terms and move forward with her life. She stayed out of the dating scene not wanting to replace the memory of Ellis with anyone, but Brody had broached that barrier. He was already embedded under her skin and though they agreed that what they did on the island would stay on the island, she couldn't help but wonder what would happen if they didn't set that limitation now knowing that they both lived in Houston.

Before she thought too long and hard about it, Kimara knew she was going to have to walk away. The history they shared would always be there and she couldn't second guess what that could eventually do to anything they tried to hold on to beyond their time on the island. They wouldn't be able to exist without the reminder of their mutual loss.

Closing her laptop, Kimara went into her bedroom and prepared for a long, hot soak in the tub. She had a lot to think about.

**

Brody relaxed out on his patio and enjoyed the afternoon breeze, though it was a heated breeze because of the extremely hot day, he loved the peace and quiet of the moment. He'd been busy since the moment he landed on the island and this was the first time he'd taken the time to sit back and relax. A bottle of his favorite beer sat on the table beside him as he stretched his legs out in front of him and took in the view of the few people who sat on the beach. He needed this time after the amorous night and morning of making love to Kimara. Even now that she was back at her place, his body hardened thinking about her luscious body and the way she responded to him each time he reached for her. Their lovemaking was magical and stirred his body in a way that he was still feeling.

After Kimara left, he was planning to go to the gym at the resort and workout, something he hadn't done since arriving on the island. At home, he worked out every day. He didn't see a need while on vacation. He was taking a break from everything he considered a norm.

Instead, he decided to enjoy a lazy day and get out to do a little shopping to get a few gifts for his family, especially Journee. He missed her most of all. He didn't like being away from her and couldn't wait to get back to see her little round face. She was a mirror image of her mother and had taken on her sweet personality even though her mother had been gone since her birth.

The night before, he'd share some of Journee's antics with Kimara and they laughed at how in charge Journee thought she was. The way he told the stories, Kimara told him it appeared that Journee was in charge. They had talked about her desire to have children of her own, but so far, that had not happened for her. He could sense she wanted to share more, but didn't and he decided not to pry.

As he sipped his beer, he thought back to the incredible nigh they'd shared. Kimara was everything, plus more. The way they seemed to be in sync, automatically knowing what they each liked and loved was something he hadn't counted on. Yes, he had wanted her from the moment he saw her and knew that any hotblooded man would, but Kimara was more than what was on the inside. He could imagine himself being involved with her beyond what they were sharing on the island, but he knew that wasn't to be. They had agreed to enjoy the time they had left on the island and that was it. Even now, he regretted agreeing to that. How was he going to walk away from a woman he felt like he had already fallen in love with? He was thinking of reconsidering the idea and wondered, now that they knew they lived in the same city, could they be more? He started to think harder about the possibility when his thoughts were interrupted by the ringing of his cell phone.

Grabbing it, he was happy to see that it wasn't his sister or mother calling him for the millionth time to be sure he was having fun and not doing any work as he had promised. Instead, it was Nelson.

"What's up, man!" he said answering.

"I was calling to ask you the same thing. How is the island life treating you?" Nelson asked.

"This place is all that. You need to bring your wife down here for a week. She would think you were king of the world!" Brody exclaimed.

"That good, huh? I may have to do that. I know you've been there a few days and I wanted to let you know everything back here at home is going great. Journee is spending the night with us tonight. I thought I'd give your mother a break and bring my goddaughter over here to hang with her godbrothers. Besides, Amelia is still trying to put her bid in for another child, hoping for a daughter. These two boys give her the blues and I think she's ready for a little girl to dress up all pretty and balance out the male to female ratio around here," Nelson laughed.

"Ah, y'all are thinking about another baby? Man, Peyton and I were planning to have a whole house full of kids, but things didn't work out that way. Journee loves being an only child and having me all to herself."

"Hey, bro, don't count yourself out just yet. One day when you stop playing that friends with benefits game, you'll settle down and find that perfect woman for you and Journee. You'll still get that house full of kids you always wanted. You know Peyton is in heaven angry at you for holding so tight to her memory that you won't allow yourself to get serious about a woman. I'm holding out hope for you, my brother!" Nelson laughed.

"Yeah, well you keep that hope alive," Brody jested. "Is Journee there now?"

"No, Amelia took her to the nail salon to get matching pink nails or something. I don't know. All I know is she left me here at home with these two wild boys and the only reason you don't hear mayhem happening in the background is because they're eating. Are you holding up your end of the deal and enjoying your time away?" Nelson asked.

Brody's thoughts immediately turned to Kimara. Because of her, he was having the time of his life. Though they'd had the most incredible sexual experience, it was the after-sex talk that he loved the most.

He enjoyed talking about sports and loved that they were both, not just from Texas, but from Houston and shared a love for their Texas teams. He was a huge Baltimore Ravens fan since one of his college buddies played on the team and she loved the Philadelphia Eagles.

He and Kimara had ended up talking for the rest of the

night until they made love once again when the sun started coming up and they'd finally grabbed a couple of hours of sleep. He knew that Kimara was planning on doing some shopping with some friends she'd met on the island and he was taking some time to himself. Thoughts of her were not far from his mind.

"I am enjoying it more than I thought I would."

"Well, I hope that means no work and a lot of women. There's a lot you can do in a couple of days and can leave behind when you come back to Texas. Oh, to be single and in your shoes!" Nelson proclaimed.

"Right. Don't even go there. You know you wouldn't give up your life with Amelia for this single life I'm living for anything. Trust me, I would trade places with you in a heartbeat."

Brody realized what he'd said and didn't want Nelson to feel bad because of him not having Peyton anymore while he still had his wife to love on all the time.

"I know you would. I hate what happened to you and Journee."

"I know, so do I, but it's been five years and I'm in a much better place than I was back then."

"Think you'll ever want to get married again?" Nelson asked.

Brody hadn't thought about that, but hoped that one day he would marry again and bring into his and Journee's life a woman who would love his daughter like her own. As if fate had a hand in his thoughts, he looked up and saw Kimara wave at him from the other side of the locked gate that led to his villa. Her presence was unexpected, but very much wanted.

"Nelson, I need to jet," he said.

"Alright. Let's get in a game of basketball when you get back and you can tell me about all the ways you made the best of your time on the island and don't think of leaving out any antics with island women. You know I have to live the single man's life vicariously through you," Nelson laughed.

"Yeah, whatever. Kiss my daughter for me. I'll catch up with you when I get back."

Brody hung up the phone and hopped up to open the gate for Kimara. Hey hadn't made plans to connect until later in the evening. He hoped everything was okay.

Chapter 14

Kimara waved nervously at Brody as he stood to greet her. She wasn't planning to see him until later when they agreed to have dinner together. Once she come across their connection via the internet search she had done, she couldn't take her mind off of it and wanted to talk to him about it. They had talked about many things, but neither mentioned the loss of their spouse or how it had happened. That time had been devastating for her and no doubt it had been for Brody as well. She wanted him to know what she knew and they could decide how or if they would continue their time together. She hoped she didn't ruin the little time they had left by bringing up a time she was sure he would like to leave in the past.

"Hello, beautiful!" Brody said as he greeted her at the gate just before opening it. Before she could reply, he kissed her passionately and the feelings from the night before flooded through her. She was amazed at how familiar her body had already become with him.

"Hi. I hope I'm not disturbing you. I know we didn't have any plans to see each other until later, but I wanted to talk to you about something. I knew you said you were planning to sit out and enjoy the daylight and I took a chance on walking by hoping you would still be out here. It's a beautiful day for enjoying the sun," she said.

"Yes, it is and it's even more beautiful now that you're here. I thought you were doing some shopping."

"I was and I will. I wanted to talk to you about something and it couldn't wait," she said.

Brody's antenna went up and he sensed something was wrong.

"Is everything okay?" he asked. "Come on and sit out here with me," he said as they walked back to the patio. He pointed to the lounge chair for Kimara to have a seat and he sat on the other, facing her. The look on her face told him that whatever she wanted to talk about, must be pretty serious. Perhaps, she was having second thoughts about what they shared and was going to let him down easy. The idea set his nerves on edge. He thought they shared something special or at least that was the vibe he'd been feeling all night. Unlike him, Kimara appeared to be troubled by something and since she was coming to talk to him, it had to be about him or perhaps their time together. What bothered him most was her efforts to not making eye contact with him.

"I'm sorry to drop in on you like this," Kimara said, clearly stalling as she gathered her words carefully.

"What's wrong? Talk to me," he said. Whatever the issue was, he wanted her to get it out so that he could respond. He could tell her behavior wasn't as jovial as it had been whenever he saw her. He wasn't sure of what to make of the sullen tone of her words and her demeanor was not one that was as inviting as she had been since they met. Something was wrong. He sat in silenced as he watched Kimara look around as if expecting someone to show up.

"Do you want to go inside and talk or is out here okay? I was enjoying a beer and could get you one or perhaps a glass of wine?" he said, trying to help her relax.

"No, I'm good and let's sit out here. It's a beautiful day."

Brody slid his lounge chair over closer to hers to try and encourage her to relax and talk.

"What's wrong, Kimara? You're making me nervous. Is this about last night? Are you having regrets?" he asked, not wanting to wait to find out what was on her mind. He felt a need to pull it out of her.

Kimara looked at him shocked. The last thing she wanted was for Brody to think that she had regrets about their night together. It was one of the best of her life.

"No, not at all. Last night and this morning were wonderful and I have no regrets whatsoever. Let me explain why I'm here so that you won't have to guess. Well, let me start by saying I wasn't trying to pry into your life beyond what you were sharing with me. It's just that I was curious about you because you're the first man in a long time that I find myself interested in and it's not just about the great sex, though that was amazing," she said smiling and blushing.

"That's good to know. I aim to please," Brody joked, trying to lighten the mood.

Kimara smiled and this time she looked him in the eyes and he could sense her hesitation about something.

"I was thinking about you earlier and I took out my laptop and googled you," she admitted.

Brody relaxed.

"There's nothing about me to hide and I hope you didn't

come across something that made you uncomfortable. I'm an open book and if you felt the need to google me, then you should have," he said.

"I know and I don't want you to think I was trying to pry. You intrigue me. I didn't find anything that made me uncomfortable. I actually found something that connects you and I," she said.

"Something that connects us? Something like what?" he asked. Now, he was the one intrigued. What about him could she have found that they had in common?

Kimara reached into her bag and pulled out two printed pieces of paper. She handed him the first one and held on to the other.

Brody took the paper Kimara held out to him and opened it. The first thing he spotted on the page was a picture of Peyton and the story about the train crash. Seeing the article, his heart practically stopped. What did Peyton have to do with her?

"If I overstepped, please tell me and I'll apologize profusely," Kimara said.

"No, not at all. I know I didn't tell you that I lost my wife. I wasn't hiding it. It's not a subject I often discuss with anyone."

"I know. Are you upset that I found this? I really didn't mean to pry," Kimara said.

"No, it's okay. What I don't understand is you said that we had something that connected us. What does this article and picture of Peyton have to do with that?" he asked and waited curiously.

"I know you never told me about your wife and I never told you about my husband. In fact, I never told you that I had once been married," she said.

"You were?" he said, surprised. They hadn't talked about relationships or spouses. They had asked each other if they had a significant other back at home and neither had. After that, all talk of others went out the window.

"Yes, I was and that's where we're connected in a strange way," she said.

Brody looked at her perplexed.

"I don't understand," he said.

Kimara opened the other piece of paper and handed it to him. She held her breath as she watched for his reaction to seeing a picture of Ellis.

Brody wasn't sure he was still breathing in and out as he read an article similar to the one about Peyton. He looked up and over at Kimara before going back to the article.

"Your husband, Ellis, died in the same crash that killed Peyton," he said softly.

"Yes, he did. Five years this week, I lost him."

Brody sat stunned as he read the article and wondered what the odds could be of them having been through the same experience and then not only ending up on the island at the same time, but finding each other and having the kind of vibe they shared. When he stopped reading, he looked over at Kimara. He could sense in her restless body movement that she was nervous about what his reaction would be.

"You're right, there is a connection. I don't remember you from all the media surrounding this. I retreated away from the spotlight and focused on Journee after being told Peyton wouldn't make it," he explained.

"I'm sorry if my prying brought up bad memories for you,

but I couldn't believe it when I read the article. What are the odds that you and I would run across each other here, on this island, far away from Texas after going through the exact same experience years ago?"

Brody, still stunned, was at a loss for words and if he never thought he would ever feel closer to Kimara than he had over the past two days, he was wrong. Putting the papers aside, he leaned over and took her by the hands and looked into her eyes.

"It wasn't a chance meeting, it was fate. I'm not the strongest religious man in the world, but I believe in a higher power and our paths crossing had a reason. I don't know what it is, but I do know that in a split second, I feel closer to you than I did five minutes ago. Does knowing this change what we're sharing while on the island?" he asked.

Kimara looked deeper into his eyes.

"I don't want it to change. I've enjoyed spending time with you, which is why I wanted you to know. We've had the same pain, suffering the same loss and we're also here on this island at the same time. I don't know what it means. The only thing I know right now is that I want to continue to spend my time left on the island with you. I don't want that to change. I still think that when we leave, we should leave what we shared here on the island. I know we haven't talked in depth about this, but I'm having the time of my life, but reality awaits me back home and if I have these last few days on this island with you, I don't want anything to interrupt what we are sharing."

Brody exhaled, happy to hear that Kimara wasn't full of regret from the night before and that she was still open to the time they had left and making the best of it. He couldn't think of anything he wanted more than being with her.

"Come here," Brody said and pulled Kimara to her feet. Leaning back on the lounge chair, he threw his legs over each side and sat Kimara between them with her back to his chest so that he could enclose her in his embrace. The moment she was comfortably against him and leaned her head back onto his shoulder, he moved her hair to the side which was flowing down around her shoulders and kissed her sweetly behind the ear.

"I don't want either of us to think of anything negative or anything that would take up our time that we have left. Let's focus on having fun and not focus on what brought either of us here. We're here and we're enjoying each other. How does that sound?" he said holding her close.

Kimara encircled Brody's arms with hers and held on to him as tightly as he was holding on to her. He made her feel so good when they were close like this and he was right, now that their past was out in the open, they shouldn't focus on things that made them sad. They needed to focus on each other and what that meant for now.

"Sounds like a plan."

"Listen, let's lighten the mood, okay? There is a game night happening in one of the lounges tonight. From what I understand, there are board games, card games and even a room for video game competitions, though that's not my lane. What do you say we go have some fun and play some games? I, myself, am a master at spades," Brody said. He really did want to change the subject off of anything heavy and get back to enjoying their time while on the island.

"I love playing spades and just about any other card game. I say, let's do it," Kimara agreed and smiled when Brody's arms tightened around her. She melted back into him, happy that her snooping didn't ruin what they were sharing. Before long, she felt the need for him burn through her as it had the night before. They had a few hours before the game night and she wasn't ready to go back to her room.

"We'll partner up and put a hurting on anyone who challenges us in spades!" Brody declared.

"I'm all for that. In the meantime, did you have any other plans that I'm interrupting?" she asked.

"None. You have something in mind?" he asked.

Kimara wiggled her hips against him and the moment she felt him rise to the occasion, she knew she didn't have to lay out for him why she was asking.

"Mmm. We have a few hours and I think we can figure out something to do with the time."

Kimara giggled when Brody stood and picked her up in his arms and carried her inside. The best idea she'd had all day was coming to his room.

Chapter 15

Stretching and reaching across the bed to pull Kimara closer to him, Brody was surprised to find the other side of the bed empty. He'd fallen asleep after they returned to Kimara's villa where they enjoyed some quiet time talking before heading into the bedroom. They were having a hard time keeping their hands and other body parts off of each other to his delight.

Noticing darkness still covered the night and the bedroom was in total darkness, he knew it wasn't yet daytime and he wondered why Kimara wasn't in bed. Sitting up, he looked around the bedroom and didn't see her anywhere. Slipping out of bed, he knew she couldn't have gone far and slipped on the jeans he'd had on earlier.

Walking into the living room area, he found Kimara standing out on the patio looking out at the ocean. Something must be on her mind if she was out here and not in bed next to him.

"Kimara? Is everything okay? I reached for you and you weren't there," he said coming up behind her.

"I didn't mean for my absence to wake you. It's still the middle of the night," she said.

"I like having you in bed with me. I woke up and the room seemed empty without you. Is everything okay?" he asked.

"I'm leaving in a few hours," she said somberly.

Kimara had been so consumed with enjoying their time together the past few days, that her last day had snuck up on them and reality had set in. Their time together was ending in a few short hours when she would head to the airport for her flight home. Brody still had one additional day, but she was leaving and she already felt empty. She was going to miss him.

"I know. I've thought about that all day. In a few hours, I'll have to let you go and I don't want to. I know we agreed to enjoying each other while we are here without making any demands beyond these few days, but I want you to know I'm going to miss you. Our time together is more than I could have ever imagined and I'm not sure I can just turn it off. What if we thought about time beyond the island?" he asked, hopeful. Brody hadn't shared his thought with Kimara about the possibility of them continuing to see each other when they returned to Houston. What they were enjoying was more than sex on an exotic island. They were having the kind of relationship that people build lives around. He had fallen in love with Kimara and didn't want to let her go. He didn't want to bring down the mood by focusing on that, but he felt that coming all this way and eventually finding each other wasn't supposed to end after a week – it wasn't.

"I'm going to miss you, too and I don't know how to handle that, so when I realized I couldn't sleep, I came out here. This view is so incredible and it will be hard giving this view up to go back to life in Houston. No Brody and no view leaves me feeling empty and lonely already," Kimara admitted.

"That's how I felt when I reached for you and all I got was air. We don't have to let this end because we're going back home. We both live in Houston and I know we're considering this an island fling and we wanted to focus on the fun of being here and not the reality of going back home, but now that we are confronted with that reality, we're two adults who don't have to walk away if we don't want to," he said.

When Kimara hesitated with her response, he knew what was on her mind.

"This time with you has been intense and I don't want you to think I haven't enjoyed it because I have. Every minute has been amazing, but I don't know if I'm ready for the reality of it when I get back home. I can't imagine that what happened five years ago won't come up and somehow be a crutch in anything we would like to have together. I'm not sure I'm strong enough to handle the impact of that right now. I want to, I really want to, but I'm not sure I'm ready. We both lost our spouses in that crash and that's always going to be the elephant in the room. I haven't had luck in talking much about it to anyone. The memories have kept me from a lot of things and you caught me off guard. You made me feel things I haven't felt in a long time and I don't know what that will be like when I get back home. At the end of the day, now that I know how we are connected, I can't stop thinking about that either. I don't want to walk away and not look back, but deep down, I feel like I need to in order to move forward. That crash has had me bound for so long that I can't have anything about that time as a constant reminder if I'm to move on with my life. Knowing what we share when it comes to that is going to be too much," she admitted.

Brody exhaled and knew he needed to tread lightly. Their loss had been great, but he was a believer that they could build something if they learned to move forward and he wanted to do that together. He wasn't ready to let go.

"No one may be able to understand what you're saying more than me. How long are you going to let the past keep you from the present?" he asked.

"I know, but what's happening here with you isn't something I expected or planned on and now, knowing the past the we share, I can't seem to focus beyond our time here. What's that going to look like knowing the pain we both suffered?"

"Baby, maybe what we need to do is talk through our feelings about what happened that day five years ago. Maybe we need to share our deepest hurdles in dealing with how or lives changed. That may help us both move on to see if what we are sharing here is worth pursuing once we get back home. You're leaving in a few hours and I have one more full day. We have time to figure out if what we're feeling for each other is worth fighting through the past to see if we could have any kind of future."

"I hear what you're saying and it's all happening so fast. I've never fallen for anyone as fast as I've fallen for you. I don't know how to handle that. What we've been sharing was supposed to be a fling for a few days, not involving feelings or thoughts of what we'll do back in the states. I wasn't ready for that and now that we're about to face it, I'm hesitant to go beyond the original intent. Doesn't it scare you that our past could come in between what we could possibly have together? It terrifies me," Kimara said in what sounded to her as a pleading voice. In her head, she was pleading with

Brody to understand her reservations. She cared deeply for him and wasn't sure she could handle anything beyond the island not working because she still couldn't let go of the past.

"Yes, it terrifies me, too. I, like you, didn't come here with the notion that I would find someone I would want to see beyond the few days of being here, but that's exactly what happened. I don't know where we go from here, but you know what, we don't really have to decide this now or even tomorrow. If we're meant to be more to each other than what we've shared, then it will happen. I don't want to cloud our last night together with anything other than holding you in my arms and making love to you until we fall asleep with exhaustion. Come back to bed with me," Brody said.

Kimara turned around after hearing the deep emotion in his voice. From the moonlit sky she could see the hurt in his face and the sullen mood that now hovered above them. She didn't want that. She loved being in his arms and he had come to mean a lot to her in a few short days. Tonight, all she wanted to do was feel. Their time together has been magical and she didn't want that magic to end, not tonight.

She took Brody's hand in hers and walked back inside, locking the door behind them. When she reached the bed's edge, unsnapped his jeans and removed them from his body. She then removed the thin robed she had on and turned them so that he was against the bed. Giving him a slight nudge, Brody sat down on the edge. She didn't want words tonight. All she wanted was for them to feel. If this was all that she would have as a reminder of him, she wanted to make it last as if it were a lifetime.

Leaning forward, she placed a soft open mouth kiss on his

chest and listened as he exhaled and enjoyed the intimacy of the kiss. It wasn't rushed or hurried, but slow and deliberate as she used her mouth to make love to his. She took great care in making sure Brody knew they weren't in a rush and that this last night together was important to her.

As her need for him grew frantic, she grabbed one of the condoms that rested on the nightstand and slipped it on his hardened flesh, already standing long and hard, waiting for her. She didn't know what the future held, but for now, she was living her life in this moment and nothing could take the place of how powerful and strong Brody felt as she moved up and down on him. Grasping on to his shoulders, they didn't speak, but she could read his pleasure all over his face. She kept her eyes locked on his, where she may have thought to close them in order to focus on feeling. She no longer had to do that. Being with Brody was a tantalizing feeling that fulfilled every need she could ever want from an intimate connection with a man. This is what she wanted to remember about her time on the island – her and Brody locked together and pure bliss.

Brody knew the time for words was over and all he and Kimara needed to do was give each other this last night of feeling. As he held her in his arms as she sat astride him and moved her body in a way that had him teetering on the edge of a powerful release, he leaned his head forward and suckled her breasts. The moment he did, Kimara moved faster on top of him and as she surged down, he used long, powerful strokes up into her using the foundation his feet made with the floor to control their movement. He loved that the only sounds heard in the room were of their bodies grappling together and their soft moans of pleasure. This was a sound he was going to miss. The sounds had never had the impact on his body the way they had coming from Kimara. He was in love, there was no doubt about that. Even though they had only been together a few days, he knew when she was close. He could feel it in the way she was riding him and when her breath became ragged, he held tighter to her hips and gave her all he had. Kimara's screams of pleasure reached him as his orgasm shot through his body while Kimara was in the throes of hers. Together they moaned and groaned through the mutual gratification. Stronger than any orgasm he had ever had before, he felt the moment Kimara's second orgasm flowed through her causing him to pump wildly as a second eruption slayed him and threw him into a wild frenzy, barely able to hold on to her as she bounced on his lap, calling his name over and over again.

Brody had never experienced one orgasm after another and he felt like he was floating as he screamed and held on to her with all of his might.

"I love you, Kimara," he shouted as he continued to ride the wave of pleasure that had now overpowered him. He was a goner.

Chapter 16

Kimara made her way through the airport to get her luggage, distracted and paying no attention to anything going on around her. She'd slept on the return flight after leaving Brody at the airport. He still had one more day before returning home and she already missed his handsome face. They didn't exchange a lot of conversation when they woke in the morning as he helped her pack for her return trip. The idea of what her leaving meant was as large as an elephant in the room, but neither spoke about what was next. They had talked briefly about it the night before while standing on the patio and they silently agreed to not bring it up again. Brody had said if anything was meant to be, it would be, but she was hesitant. As much as she missed and wanted him, she didn't want to ruin what they could have because she was still stuck in the past. She thought she was able to now let go and that was the purpose for her trip. She wasn't so sure in her mind she was ready even though her body was giving her all kinds of signals that it was time for her to move on to the next phase of her life and possibly with Brody.

The plan for her trip was to get away, have some fun and

then get back to life which she was doing. What she hadn't planned on was the strong feelings she had for Brody. What she also hadn't expected was for him to scream out that he loved her. She wasn't sure if it was because of the intimate moment or if he had really fallen in love with her. She was afraid to admit it to herself, but she had fallen in love with him and it scared her. She was terrified of what that meant.

How could she fall in love with a man after a few days of being with him? Unable to say the words out loud, she knew the reality was that she was in love. Brody was everything any woman could ask for and he treated her like a precious jewel. He adored her and never missed a chance to tell her how beautiful she was, words every woman wanted to hear. She knew love and what it felt like. What she was feeling for him wasn't something fly-by-night. It was real and she was scared of her feelings.

Kimara remembered when she had first begun dating Ellis and how it had taken her months to actually fall in love with him. With Brody, it happened in days and to be truthful, it may have happened the first day – the first time she'd laid eyes on him. The thought frightened her. Was it really love she was feeling or had she gotten caught up in the intimacy they shared and gotten it confused with love? Only time would tell, she thought as an image of his face came into view. She missed him terribly and it had only been a few hours. Her mind was so focused on Brody that she didn't see her sister rushing toward her until she was practically up on her. Before she could speak any kind of greeting, Casey grabbed her into a bear hug and wouldn't let go.

"I'm glad you're home. I missed you. Next time, take me with you," Casey said.

"Right, like your better half would go for you being on an exotic island without him!" Kimara chimed. "I missed you!" he added.

"I missed you, too. I don't like you gone for this much time, but I know you needed it. Let's find your luggage while you tell me about the great time you had. Did you have the best time of your life on this trip? What about that guy you met? Did anything happen? Did you have a fling with an island guy? You know someone who helped you get back on that horse and I do mean back on it!" Casey shouted and then covered her mouth when she realized how loud she was being.

Kimara laughed at the millions of questions being tossed her way with no intention of answering any of them. She playfully slapped Casey on the arm and turned back around to keep an eye out for her bag so that it wouldn't pass by her a second time.

"Sis, you play too much. I thought you were going to be in the car waiting," Kimara said. "I think I missed my luggage," she added as she saw some luggage pass by her for a second time.

"I was, but I couldn't wait to see you and instead of sibling violence, you should be giving me the best sister hug in the world because I missed you and I know you missed me!" she shouted as others looked on.

Kimara turned back around and quickly hugged her.

"I'll hug you better after my luggage comes back around again. I let it slip by me and I didn't feel like racing to the other end to grab it, so give me a minute before you plunge into fifty questions about my trip," Kimara said.

"Ugh, you're so frustrating. You can multi-task like no one

else I've ever met and I think you can look for luggage and spill the juicy details to your one and only sister, please?" Casey begged.

When Kimara turned around, she laughed at Casey who was swaying and bouncing like a child who was waiting for a parent to take them outside to play.

"Okay, come closer," Kimara said.

"I'm all ears."

"I had a great time. I told you about the excursions and the partying I did and I also played cards and other board games. I tried a few new drinks and even got in some swimming. You know the water is crystal clear and blue. It's actually blue and beautiful, especially at night."

Before she could continue, Casey interrupted her.

"Okay, enough of the fluff stuff, what about the island men or better yet that guy you told me about? Did you temporarily change your name to Stella? You know from that movie with Taye Diggs?"

"Girl, stop it! My name is still Kimara and now I did not have a Stella and Winston moment. I did, however, spend a lot of time with the guy I mentioned when we talked."

"I knew it!" Casey said loud enough that a large group of people standing around turned and looked at them.

Kimara saw her luggage and ignored Casey's loud excitement.

"Can you be any louder?" Kimara said grabbing her two suit cases before the belt moved them out of her reach. As soon as she had them, she started walking without knowing where Casey had parked.

"Who is this guy?" Casey asked as they walked.

"Where is the car?"

"Who is this guy?" Casey said again.

"Casey, focus. Where is the car? I'm exhausted and I want to go home. We can talk in the car so that you don't scream out my business to everyone in the airport. Let's go," Kimara said.

"This way," Casey said and took them in a new direction.

As they walked, Kimara was thankful for the silence while she contemplated how much to tell Casey. Her sister could be overbearing, but on the other hand, she was the one person she could tell everything to and she was anxious to tell her about Brody. After a few short moments of maneuvering, they were in the garage and she could see Casey's car a few feet away.

After getting her luggage loaded and finally settled into the car, Kimara laid the seat back and rested her eyes. The entire time she was on the island, she was nearly as exhausted as she was now. The excitement and fun she had on the island made her forget how tired she should have been from the lack of sleep. Now, the weight of her exhaustion settled over her and she barely remembered the ride to her house.

Chapter 17

Brody entered his mother's house to the sound of little feet running at a high rate of speed toward him. Dropping his bags to the hardwood floor of the entryway, he braced himself for Journee's leap into his arms. She didn't disappoint when she freely leaped and he caught her mid-air.

"You're home!" Journee shouted.

"Yes, and I missed you the most," Brody said, kissing her all over her face to her delight.

"I missed you the most, Daddy!"

"Did you bring me a present?" Journee asked.

"I'm your present," he said and knew it wouldn't be enough.

"Auntie Brynne and Nana said you were going to bring me a present back if I was a good girl. I was really good even when I was at aunt Amelia and uncle Nelson's house. The boys were bad and got in trouble, but not me. You can call and ask. Can I have my present now?" Journee asked.

Brody knew she wouldn't stop with sharing with him the accolades of how good she was while he was gone until he gave her a present. Setting her back down on her feet, he reached for the big bag he'd sat on the floor.

"This big bag is for you," he said and handed it to her. He watched as Journee sat down on the floor and started going through the bag. His last day on the island, he'd had enough time to finally get some shopping done. He had to fill his time left once Kimara left. He didn't realize how much he had come to depend on seeing her and being with her until she was gone and he was on the island without her. His last night had been a lonely one.

He tried going out and joining in on his last guest gathering, but it wasn't the same. He couldn't stop thinking about how much he already missed Kimara and the fact that they had not resolved what the future could hold for them. He should have pushed harder for her to reconsider something more long-term with him. He thought they would have discussed it especially after he blurted out that he loved her. He knew she heard it and he remembered saying it. It wasn't something said only in the heat of the moment, but it was a declaration that had been on the tip of his tongue since the first moment. He could no longer hold it in. Sadly, they didn't talk about it and he let it go. He didn't want her to have more to deal with along with the internal struggle about them he knew she was already having.

"What did you bring me, big brother?" Brynne said walking up to him followed by his mother. He hugged each of them and looked around for his father.

"He's not here. He had a meeting at school that ran over," his mother said.

His father often had meetings that ran over when he held meetings with the professors at the college where he served as the department head of the English department.

"I'll catch him later. I'm tired and all I want to do is go

home and spend some quiet time with Journee."

"Quiet time?" Brynne asked. "Have you met your daughter? She's a non-stop talker. You won't get any rest because she wants to tell you about every aspect of her day while you were gone."

"That's fine, too. I missed her and I'm glad to be home. I'm sure work has piled up while I was away and I'm hoping to catch up on a little of it before I head back to work in a few days."

"Wait, what? You didn't get any work done while you were gone? I know you and I also know that you took a briefcase full of work with you on that trip. When I checked on your house, I noticed the briefcase was obviously missing from your home office. You promised to have fun."

Brody let his sister finish her rant before explaining.

"Are you finish chastising me? Now, I said I was going to have fun and not focus on work and I did that. I didn't take the briefcase with me on the trip. I stopped by the office before heading to the airport and I had it with me. I promise, I left it in the car at the airport the whole time," Brody explained.

Brody handed Brynne a bag and then another to his mother.

"Oh, you didn't have to, but I'm glad you did."

"Don't be too excited. Everything in the bag isn't for you, so take it home and look through it."

"Gotcha," she said.

"Did you have a good time, son?"

"I had the best time, mom. This trip was exactly what I needed. I feel refreshed, almost like a new man."

"That's good to know. Are you sure you want to take

Journee with you? I'm heading to a meeting at the church and I can take her with me if you want to go home and rest."

"I'm good, mom. I'll take her with me."

"Okay, well I'm glad you're back and I'm running late. One of you lock up when you leave. Call me later and fill me in on your trip," she said and left.

Brody watched Journee open one package after the other as her excitement grew with each present she opened. He was happy he was able to find a store that wrapped everything for her. One thing he loved was watching her open up gifts that were covered with wrapping paper. He found that as exciting as the look on her face when she finally set eyes on what was inside. He also noticed that Brynne was unusually quiet and he turned toward her and was faced with a crazy look.

"What's wrong with your face?" he asked.

"Something happened on that island didn't it? What was it? You did more than have fun; you had fun and you know exactly what I mean," Brynne said and cut an eye over to Journee. She didn't want to say sex.

"What?" Brody said, trying to brush her off.

"Don't even try it. You know I can read you like a book and I remember you saying a woman's name once while we were talking on the phone," she said.

"Stop twinning me, Brynne."

Brody smiled when she feigned being hurt.

"Twinning? I'm not twinning you. I'm looking at a man who came back from a vacation on an island made for romance and all he's doing is smiling, smiling and smiling some more and I can't help it if as your big sister and twin, I can read you like a book."

"You're only three minutes older than me and I hate when you try to read me."

"So, you're saying I'm wrong and that goofy smile and over the top happiness has nothing to do with a woman? All I want to know is was it an island fling or something more?" she asked.

"I'm not admitting to anything. I already said I had a good time and I don't think you need to know any details beyond that," he said.

"You tell me everything! Why not this?" she pleaded.

Brody looked over at Journee who was enthralled with all of her presents and he leaned in closer to Brynne and exhaled. He didn't want Journee to hear their conversation. There was something said for twins who were as close as they were. She could tell when something made him happy and when something made him sad.

The day of the train crash, he remembered the conversation they had later that night after finding out that Peyton was involved in the accident. Brynne had called before he had a chance to call her and she told him she sensed something bad had happened and she wanted to check on him. That's when he told her what happened. In all the craziness, he hadn't had a chance to call his mother and sister, but Brynne knew there was a disturbance with him, something they had been able to pick up from each other over the years.

"Okay, there was a woman and no, she wasn't from the island. I met her the first day and we spent days doing things I never thought I'd do. We went skydiving, deep-sea diving, dancing several times, water skiing, snorkeling, parasailing and for the first time, I tried sushi and I loved it," he admitted.

Brynne looked around and Brody wondered what was going on.

"What's the matter with you? What are you looking for?" he asked.

"I'm looking for my conservative brother who never does anything exciting that doesn't involve an activity with his daughter. I need to meet this woman and thank her for making you enjoy your time away. So, was this just an island fling or is it more?"

"What do you mean? I've always been adventurous and yes, it was just an island fling," Brody lied and turned his attention back to Journee. He knew that Brynne would be able to read that he was lying if she could see his face.

"Liar!"

"What?"

Brody tried to sound convincing, but should have known better with his sister.

"You're lying. She's more than an island fling. You don't do anything casual which is why you haven't gotten involved seriously with anyone since Peyton died. This woman was something special. Who is she and when are you seeing her again? Anytime you need to take a trip to visit her, I'll keep Journee for you. Now spill."

"Okay, her name is Kimara and it was a fling because we agreed to leave the time we shared on the island. There is no need to fly anywhere to meet her because it's over. Besides, she lives right here in Houston."

"Are you serious? You go all the way to Turks and Caicos and you meet an incredible woman who has you smiling like a Cheshire cat only to find that she lives in the same city? I have got to meet this woman. Are you going to see her again?"

"I don't know. That's up to her, though we agreed on the island that we wouldn't. We had fun and now it's over."

"That must have been some woman because the way you're lighting up while you're talking about her tells me she was and is more than the days spent on the island. You know you can be honest with me," Brynne said.

"I know, but I don't know how to take where we left off with things. For me, it's still up in the air. She was having a hard time figuring out what she wanted and I let her go without pushing for more. There is so much more to her than her being a woman I met on vacation. I had an unbelievably good time with her and in a short amount of time, she got under my skin. I can't seem to shake it and I'm not sure I want to. The ball was in her court and she chose to walk away, not because she didn't enjoy her time with me, but because she was struggling with her past and how our pasts intertwined."

"What? I don't understand. You knew each other before the island trip?" Brynne asked.

Brody braced himself for the explanation he was about to give her.

"Brynne, she lost someone in the same train crash that took Peyton's life. Her husband died that day and I believe because of that, once we return to our lives, that fact will stand out like a sore thumb. On the island, we agreed to leave that all in Texas and just enjoy the time away. Being back home, we're forced to continue to face our pasts and she felt like they are too much alike to move beyond them and get into something more than what we had on the island. What happened to our spouses would always be in the room with us. We didn't even exchange phone numbers, emails or anything. I know her name and where she works, but that's it. She actually works for someone I know."

"A name is all you'd need to contact her. Don't tell me you're going to forget about her and move on like she didn't have a positive impact on you. You feel something for her and that's huge."

"I fell in love with her, Brynne. In less than a week, I fell in love with her and that has never happened to me before; not even with Peyton. In fact, I think I fell in love with her the first night. We spent pretty much all of our time together and anyone on the outside looking in would think we came to the island together. Our connection was off the charts and I haven't been able to stop thinking about her."

"Wow, does she know?"

"Does she know what?" he asked.

"Does she know that you love her? I know you and I know you wouldn't say that lightly and if you said it, you meant it."

"She knows. I said it, but we didn't discuss it. Things ended when she left for the airport."

"You can't let her go."

"Really, Brynne? Who does that? Who falls in love with a woman the minute he sees her?"

"Apparently, you do, so what are you waiting for? Listening to you without getting all of the details, this woman is worth going after. I can look at you and see a huge difference. I have my brother back and if this woman has something to do with you getting back to embracing life, then love is worth it. I have always been a believer in love at first sight. It's not a misnomer – love at first sight is real and when you find it, you should never walk away. Give me her name and let me see if I can find any contact information for her. I can't believe you didn't get it before you left. What were you thinking by letting her get away?"

"No, Brynne, we can't."

"Why not?"

"If she wanted to see me beyond the island, she would have given me her number, but she didn't."

"Did you ask for it?"

"No."

"There you have it. You said you know someone she works for. Why don't you reach out to that person and see if Kimara is open to seeing you now that you're back?"

"I don't know. I feel like I would be invading her personal space. If she wanted me in it, she would have said so. Instead, she said she wanted to move on because she wasn't ready to deal with more."

"You share a bond and you met each other for a reason. Trust me right now when I tell you, don't let this woman get away and not know if you could have more than what you had on the island. Think about how happy you were for those few days. I know that kind of love has been missing from your life and I'm happy to hear that you were open to being in love again and I don't care if it happened in five minutes, one hour or one day; you are in love and you shouldn't let it go. Think about that. I have to get out of here. Lock up when you and Journee leave and welcome back. I missed you like crazy. Come over to the house in a few days after you get settled back in at home."

"I will and thanks, Brynne."

"You'll think about what I said?" she asked.

"Yes, I'll think about it."

Brody hadn't been able to do anything but think about Kimara. His heart was hurting. He wanted to talk to her. He wanted to see her. He had some soul searching to do. Kimara was worth more than their time on the island. He wished he had been able to convince her of that.

"Are you ready to go, Pumpkin?" he asked Journee. As she nodded her head, he helped her pick up her presents and gather her Minnie Mouse suit case and they headed home. He had a feeling his evening would be filled with memories of what he and Kimara shared and how he could remedy how much he already missed her.

Chapter 18

"Are you humming?"

Kimora, startled, jumped at the sound of her sister's voice as she moved throughout her kitchen looking in pots and smelling the sweet aroma of southern cooking. She couldn't wait to get home and spend a few days relaxing and cooking her favorite foods. She forgot Casey was coming over and the fact that she had her own key allowed her to come and go whenever she wanted. She hadn't been expecting her though she should have.

"You scared me!" she said smiling.

"I scared you? You're scaring me right now. I thought momma was in the kitchen singing and humming and then it turned out to be you and you never do that. I had to wonder what alternate universe I was in where my sister, who has walked around in a permanent state of sadness for several years, was now singing and humming. I guess that vacation really did the trick and if I had known that, I would have suggested it earlier," Casey said.

"I have not been walking around sad for years and you know it. I have my moments, but it's not all the time and yes, the vacation was a great idea."

"Apparently it was and the only reason I left you alone about this guy you met is because you fell asleep as soon as you got in the car and I know you needed your rest. Now that we're here and mom isn't around, I want to hear about him."

Kimara was happy for the reprieve from her sister's interrogation. After getting home after her flight, she went right to her bedroom and went to sleep and Casey headed home. She needed to unwind and was happy she avoided answering a million questions. She fell asleep with Brody on her mind and when she woke up hours later, he was what she thought of first.

She missed him more than she thought she would and the feeling was almost painful. In the light of day and being back home, she wondered if she should have re-thought her decision to walk away from what they had on the island. She had slept, but it was a fitful sleep. She missed being in his arms.

"Casey, you've always been my confidant and what I don't need right now is judgment with what I'm about to share with you."

"Okay," Casey said and gave Kimara her undivided attention.

"While I was on the island, I met someone and he wasn't just someone, he was the most remarkable man I have ever met and we spent just about every moment together."

"Wait, are you telling me you....?"

No words were needed to finish that statement, so Kimara cut her off.

"Yes, that too and even that was intense and full of more craving for much more than I've ever experienced and I do mean ever."

Kimara hoped Casey was getting the message.

"You mean even more than with...?"

"Yes, and I can't believe I'm admitting that. This man was everything and I was so lost in our time together that I forgot we had just met. The way we instantly connected was crazy. We talked about any and everything and besides that, I stepped out of my comfort zone and went skydiving and deep-sea swimming. I even went ziplining and you know how boring I find golf, but he made it fun. He added a zest to my life I forgot I needed. Everything about my time with him was amazing. He treated me like I was the most precious woman in the world. When I was with him, he was focused on me. He cooked for me and catered to me. I'm telling you, he had me feeling like a queen. He helped me get out of my comfort zone as you heard from all of the activities I took part in. I even went out on a boat and had no problem laying out on the deck and enjoying the sun rays."

"Who did all that? Not my sister? Who is this superman? I need to meet him."

"I don't think that's going to happen. When we parted on the island, that was it. We went our separate ways."

Casey almost fell out of the chair with shock.

"You did what? Why?"

"We had fun and then we went back to our lives."

"You let this guy get away? This man has you around here humming and singing. You should never let him go. What happened? Did he only want an island fling? Was he married or have a girlfriend or something?"

"No, nothing like that. It was me who decided we shouldn't see each other after the island."

"Okay, then is it because he's from a state on the other side of the country and you aren't interested in something long-distance? What is it?"

Kimara hesitated and then opened up.

"He's from here in Houston. He lives right here."

"Really! You go all the way to an island on vacation and you meet the man of your dreams who happens to live right here in Houston? Oh, you shouldn't have walked away from him. That was fate, sis. You were meant to be together."

"Well, that's not all."

"There's more that will shock me? Perhaps, I need a drink first," Casey joked.

"You just may need that drink after this."

"Wait, let me get wine."

Kimara checked her pots and after turning down the fire, rejoined Casey at the counter taking a seat across from her.

"Okay, hit me with it," Casey said.

Before she could begin to explain, the intercom on the kitchen wall buzzed and Kimara reached for it.

"Yes, Oscar?" she said to the guard in the lobby of her condominium.

"Ms. Banks, there is a delivery man down here in the lobby with a large floral arrangement for you. I want to be sure it's okay to let him up or would you like to come down?" he asked.

"Flowers? Who's sending me flowers? If you confirmed where he's from, go ahead and send him up."

"Yes, Ms. Banks. I checked everything out and he's clear. I'll send him up" Oscar said.

"Thank you," she said.

"Maybe one of your clients sent them to you. You know

several companies are still trying to woo you into a lucrative consulting contract. I say let the wooing begin and hopefully it will come with a hefty dollar amount."

"I'm not starving for money and you know it. Besides, I love doing the consult work for Marjorie. This is fine for me right now until I decide what else I want to focus on. I wonder who is sending me flowers?"

"Well, we'll see soon enough."

When the door buzzer rang, Kimara opened the door to see a floral arrangement so large, she could barely see the face of the delivery man. Casey walked over and took the planter from his hands as Kimara dug around in her wallet for a tip, something the delivery guy declined to take.

"No worries. An extremely generous tip was included in the order. Have a nice day."

With that, the delivery man left and Kimara turned to see Casey searching for the card.

"If you read that before I do, I'm going to throw you out of here," Kimara joked as Casey handed her the card.

"I have never seen a more beautiful arrangement. Who are they from?" Casey asked.

Kimara opened the envelope, pulled out the card and read it to herself before reading it out loud.

"Kimara, thank you for sharing your time with me on the island. I know we agreed to walk away, but I'm hoping I can get you to join me for dinner whenever you're ready. I miss you. Brody"

Without realizing it, Kimara was smiling as bright as the hot Texas sun. She'd been home a few days and missing him and here he was sending her flowers.

"They're from Brody," she said.

"Who's Brody?"

Kimara sniffed the large bouquet. She loved flowers.

"The guy from the island I was just telling you about. How did he find me? We didn't exchange any information."

"Fate found you for him just as it did when you met him on the island. Don't question it or think too hard about it. Did he leave a number?" Casey asked.

"Yes, he left his number on the card."

"What did the card say?"

"That he misses me and wants me to call him about having dinner."

"Yes!" Casey shouted while pumping her fist in the air.

"I can't have dinner with him."

Suddenly the excitement in the air disappeared.

"Why not? You like him."

"I'm scared to."

"Why? What are you scared of."

"I'm ashamed to say I think I fell in love with him on that island and I shouldn't have," Kimara admitted.

"Don't tell me it's because of your loyalty to Ellis because if that's the case, you and I both know that Ellis loved you enough to want you to find love again if that would make you happy and right now, the way I hear you talking about this guy, this is the kind of love every woman would want to have. There is no time associated with falling in love with someone and if nothing else, you shouldn't be running away from it. Call him."

Kimara admired the beautiful arrangement and now knowing they are from Brody, she didn't expect anything but something as lovely as what she was looking at.

"I'm not ready."

"Kimmy, you are not one to slip into bed with a man and walk away from that. If I'm correct, Brody is the first man you've been intimate with since Ellis and you did that what, in a day or two? I'm not cheapening what you shared, but I know you and I know it meant something. Why are you willing to walk away from a man who clearly means more to you than just some fling on an island?"

"I don't know what to do. I fell hard for Brody, but should I have? You're right, it was only two days and we're in bed together and let me tell you, he made me feel things I've never, ever felt before. I feel like I owe more to Ellis than to replace him with another man," she said.

"Sis, you think Ellis would see it that way? He's not coming back and as much as he loved you, he would want to see you happy again and the way you have been talking to me about Brody, he sounds like an incredible man. Not many women have a chance to say they found two great men in their lifetime."

That had been the biggest struggle for her. She loved Ellis and he's gone. Not many people find love again with another remarkable man.

"I know and I've been struggling with it since I got back. I admit I miss him."

"If you feel more for this man than something casual, don't fight what you feel because of some misplaced loyalty. Be loyal to what's in your heart. Start there," Casey pleaded.

"I hear you and I know what you're saying. It's something I need to deal with and I will, just not right this moment," Kimara said and exhaled.

She didn't want to get into an argument with her sister about her feelings. She knew she was doing herself and Brody an injustice by ignoring the deep feelings she'd developed for him on the island – feelings that grew with each passing day since she'd been home.

"Okay, I'm not going to push too hard because this is something you need to do, but if this man truly is everything you just told me, you shouldn't let him get away. You were going to tell me something about him before we were interrupted by the buzzer. What was it?" Casey asked.

Kimara had forgotten all about the bomb she needed to drop.

"Oh yeah. Well, I discovered something about Brody while I was on the island. I was in my room and decided to look him up on the internet. After telling me a little more about himself, I was intrigued and you know the internet can be a magnet for the curious. I googled him and found an article about his wife," she said.

"Wife? I thought you said he wasn't married," Casey said, sounding frustrated.

"Hold on and let me finish. He's not married or at least not anymore. Five years ago, when Ellis died in the train crash, his wife was on the same train. Though Ellis died instantly, his wife was kept alive because she was pregnant and though there was no hope of her surviving, there was hope for the baby to make it. Soon after they finally delivered the baby, his wife died."

Kimara saw and felt the shock that Casey showed on her face.

"What? Are you serious?"

"Yes, I am. Can you imagine us together and that hovering

over our relationship forever? We would never be able to get beyond that."

"You can get beyond it if you want to. Perhaps you need to talk to each other about that day, share your feelings and then put your past to rest. It's time to move on and it sounds like in your heart, you want to move on with Brody. If that's the case, then do it. Give yourself the chance to be happy again. You deserve it. I'm going to say this one last thing and then I'm going to let it go. You were blessed to have Ellis for as long as you did. I know life didn't turn out the way you wanted it to and we all loved him, but he wouldn't want this life of isolation for you. The two of you had a wonderful life planned out and I remember hearing about all the plans you were making for trips, the big house in the country with animals, especially horses and then there were all the children you wanted to have. I can't help but think that he would still expect you to have that even if it means having another man that's not him to live those dreams out with."

"I know and I have done nothing but think about Brody and what we could have. Once I returned, I saw how stupid the idea of letting him go was, but now I can't go back and say I've changed my mind."

Kimara had thought many times about what life could be like for her and Brody if they hand continued what was started on the island.

"Sis, Brody sounds like an incredible guy from your description of your time together and you pushed him away because you're scared. I think he would understand your change of heart because you missed him. You're scared of the feelings you have for him and you feel like you're being unfaithful to Ellis. As much as I love you and would never want to hurt you, I'm going to say something and pray that you take this as something coming from my heart and not something to hurt or upset you. Let Ellis go. Let him rest in peace and find your new path in life. It's time for you to do it. No one expected you to go to an island and fall in love in a few days, but it sounds like you did. Now, what are you going to do about it?" Casey said.

She stood, grabbed her purse and keys and headed toward the door.

Kimara exhaled and knew Casey was saying everything she needed to hear.

"I love you," she said as she gave Casey a hug.

"Think about what I said and I'll call you later. I love you, too. Be happy."

Chapter 19

What a day, Brody thought as he began removing his clothes to get a shower and wash off his crazy day. Thankfully, the day had ended on a positive note and he was able to close on a multi-million-dollar deal for the bank within his first few days of being back to work after his vacation.

Now that he was back into the swing of things, he was settling back into his normal routine which included jumping back into work. Besides that, he was also focused on Journee's fifth birthday party which was coming up in a few weeks. Thankfully, he had his sister and mother to help him plan it. He had fielded calls and emails from Brynne all day on her ideas for the party. He was leaving most of the details up to them to handle the girlie, tea party theme, one of Journee's favorite things.

After picking her up from school, he had rushed home to make her dinner before putting on her pajamas and taking her to his parents' house to spend the night. Journee had a field trip to the zoo the next day and his mother was going as one of the chaperones.

Back at home after dropping her off, he was looking forward to a relaxing evening at home. His thoughts briefly turned to Kimara as he wondered what she'd been doing since returning home from vacation. After sending her flowers a few days ago, he had hoped she would have called him by now, but to his dismay, he hadn't heard anything. He guessed she was serious about breaking ties with him while he was suffering from missing her. How could they have shared the passion that they had and she was okay with walking away from them. Had he been the only one to feel a deep connection? He couldn't force her to give him a chance, but he hoped that she would reconsider based on the memories he knew they shared of their time together. Surely, he wasn't the only one feeling empty since they parted.

Hearing his phone chime, he grabbed for it in case it was his mother. He wondered if she was calling to tell him he forgot something when he dropped Journee off with them. Instead of seeing his mother's number, he saw a number he didn't recognize. At eight in the evening, he hoped it wasn't someone from his office since he had made it clear on many occasions that once he was off for the day, he was off and liked his down-time.

"Hello," he said answering the ringing phone.

First there was silence and then he heard a low-volume hello, so faint he could barely hear it.

"Hello?" he said again hoping the caller would speak up.

"Hi, Brody."

That time he heard her clearly and the her, was Kimara. After almost a week, she'd finally called him.

"Hi, Kimara."

"Did I catch you at a bad time?"

"No, not at all. How are you? I'm glad you called. I wasn't sure you ever would," he said.

"I know and I'm sorry that it took me this long to call you. The flowers were beautiful," she said.

"You're welcome. I'm glad you liked them."

Brody thought he would have heard from her sooner, but he knew how intense their time together on the island was and realized it may have been too much for her. After all, they had agreed to leave their time on the island back on the island and as much as he tried to, he couldn't. The minute he stepped off of the plane from the trip, he knew he wouldn't be able to just forget about her and the time they spent. She wasn't the only one spooked by their sudden connection and because it had been so strong, he figured it may be something they would want to pursue, but her lack of response had him thinking that he was the only one who felt that way.

"I love them. How have you been?" she asked.

"Miserable because I've been missing you like crazy. I know that wasn't part of what we decided when we parted ways, but it's an honest response. I've missed you."

"I've missed you too, Brody. You must think I'm an awful person after it's taken me this long to call you after you sent me the flowers. I should have called and thanked you when I received them. I'm sorry for that."

"Don't apologize. I didn't want to push you knowing the thoughts you shared with me about why you didn't want any contact after the island. I wanted you to know I was thinking about you and I have every day since you left. That last day for me wasn't the same without you. I went to bed that night and wanted to reach for you and hold you in my arms. In that short period of time, you came to mean so much to me."

"You're not the only one. I wake up in the night wishing

you were with me."

"It shows that the feelings we have aren't just casual," he said.

"I know that now. So, how did you get my address to send me the flowers? They brighten up my dining room," he said smiling.

"Well, I didn't actually get your address."

"You're very mysterious," she laughed.

"Not really. I remembered you telling me about the consulting firm you do work for occasionally and if you remember, I told you I knew the owner, Marjorie. I called her and didn't ask for your address, but I did ask if she would have the flowers sent directly to you as a favor and she agreed, seeing no harm done since she wasn't revealing any personal contact information. I went into the flower shop, picked out the flowers I wanted in the arrangement and when I was done, Marjorie called the shop and gave them the information they needed to send the flowers to you. I didn't want to intrude on your private space. I wanted you to know that I was thinking about you. I also hoped you were missing me as much as I was missing you. Sending the flowers was my way of letting you know I was here if you changed your mind about us," he said.

"I've missed you too, Brody. I've missed talking to you, seeing you and laying in your arms. When I came home after landing, I walked in here, looked around and for the first time in a long time, I realized just how empty this place was. The quietness was as loud as a bullhorn. In my mind, I could hear your voice and your laugh and I longed to hear both. I struggled with what to do after not feeling the pull to any man in a long, long time. Today while I was cleaning, I noticed the flowers were finally getting old and soon I would have to throw them out and that made me long to see and talk to you. I hope it's not too late to apologize."

"Again, no need to apologize for anything. What we shared on that island was incredible and it wasn't just the sex, which was amazing, but it was talking to you and having the kind of fun that we did. It made me realize that I forgot how to have that kind of fun."

"I feel the same way. Temporarily, I forgot about how sad I had been when I arrived and I was focused on living life again. I've really missed you," Kimara admitted.

"I've missed you, too. What are we going to do about all of this missing we have going on? I'd like to see you," he said.

"I want to see you, too."

"Well, it's only a little after eight. Would you like to meet me for a drink someplace?" Brody asked, hopeful.

"No."

Her response shocked him. He wasn't expecting a quick no.

"Well, how about a quick dinner at a place of your choosing?"

"No."

Brody was perplexed. She missed him and wanted to see him as much as he wanted to see her, but she didn't seem like she really wanted to see him when every time he made a suggestion, she responded with a quick no.

"Okay, what's going on here? You don't want to meet for a drink or dinner, so why don't I let you tell me what you want."

He hoped letting her be the decision maker, he could get to where she would turn her no to a yes.

"You."

Brody's body jumped with excitement. That one word spoke volumes and though he wanted nothing more than to hold her in his arms again, he didn't want to be too presumptuous.

"Me?"

"Yes, you. I want to see you."

"That's why I offered dinner or a drink. What do you suggest?" he asked.

"Brody, I don't want dinner or a drink. I just want you, tonight. I am dying without seeing and touching you and having you touch and love me. I was crazy to walk away from us and I don't want to be apart from you. I need you – just you, not a drink or dinner," she explained.

The message was loud and clear and Brody knew he was all in. He had been since the moment he met her.

"Do you want to come here or should I come there? Where would you be most comfortable?" he asked.

"Do you mind coming over here?" she asked.

"All you had to do was ask. Where am I coming to?"

Brody grabbed a pen from his briefcase to write down her address. He knew that area which had a condominium complex where he thought of making a purchase until he realized he loved having the big backyard for Journee to play in.

"You got all that?" she asked, drawing his attention back to the conversation.

"Yes. Give me thirty minutes and I'll be there."

Hanging up the phone, he raced to the shower knowing he was on a mission. He needed to make one stop on his way to her house, but that quick stop would only take a few minutes.

Nothing was going to keep him from the woman he loved. Not tonight or any other night. He wasn't letting her get away. He knew what it was like to have love and then lose it and Kimara would not be another woman that he had to let go of for any reason. Her phone call to him was all he needed. Again, fate was playing a hand in his life. Kimara happened to call on the night that Journee was with his mother, giving him a free evening. If Journee had been home, he would have to postpone his meeting with Kimara.

"Alright, if you're telling me I need to get it together and live again, I'm doing it. No more signs, okay?" Brody said to no one in particular. In his heart, he was speaking to Peyton. He was given a second chance at the kind of love he once had and now had again. Finding Kimara was proof that a love lost was not a love lost to him forever.

**

Kimara hung up her phone and looked in the mirror as she paced back and forth. Her heart was beating so fast she had to take a big gulp to slow it down. She had done it. She had called Brody, taking life by the horns and jumping in feet first to love again. She heard the words come out of her mouth, but wasn't sure she was really saying them. She let him know that without a doubt, she wanted him.

"Who are you?" she said out loud.

"When did you start being so bold as to tell a man you wanted him and then invite him over for sex?"

Well, the truth was, it wasn't about the sex. It was about picking up on what they had started on the island and going with wherever it leads. The start had to be with her since it was her decision to walk away when it was clear that Brody thought different. It was time for her to live and love again.

Brody got the message of what she meant when she said she wanted him and she also knew that he knew it was more than the physical. She was saying she wanted him, all of him. She was ready.

Brody wasn't just any man. He was an incredible man who had shown her what it meant to live again. She tried to fight it when she returned which was why she didn't call him after getting the flowers and the card with his number on it. Several times, she'd picked up her phone to call him and never completed punching in the numbers before hanging up.

Tonight, Brody was on his way and she had thirty minutes to prepare. Looking around her room, everything was already cleaned. She left her room and walked around the condo picking up items she'd left strewn about and checked to be sure she at least had a bottle of wine. She had just enough time to grab a quick shower and put on some sexy undies remembering how much Brody enjoyed taking them off of her. She loved wearing them and loved the look on Brody's face every time they were together. She wasn't sure she was ready for him when she left the island, but now she knew, she was more than ready.

It was time.

Chapter 20

Using the code that Kimara had given him for the underground garage, Brody quickly found a parking space and made his way to the bank of elevators not far away and pulled out the elevator key code that would take him to her floor. He pushed the button for the seventeenth floor which was also the top floor and waited. In a few minutes, he would see Kimara again and his heart leaped for joy. His body following the same suit didn't surprise him because he remembered every time he'd seen her while they were having fun on the island, his body longed to connect with her.

From the moment he'd heard her voice on the phone, everything changed for him. He no longer felt empty as if he'd allowed her to walk out of his life forever without fighting for the love that was blossoming. He moved with the speed of lightening, showering and getting out of the door in thirty minutes. He was anxious to hold Kimara in his arms again and make sure she knew where he was coming from. He didn't want a casual fling with her – he wanted a relationship because he believed there was more in store for them.

Exiting the elevator and with long powerful strides, he

walked up to her door, rang the bell and waited. Within a few seconds, the door opened and his heart practically leaped out of his chest at the sight of her. Just as beautiful as he remembered, he beamed when she smiled up at him. It felt like more than just a week or so since he'd last seen her, but he was much better now that she was standing in front of him. He now had confirmation that the moment he told her he loved her, it wasn't in the heat of the moment. He felt nothing but love as soon as he saw her.

"Hello, beautiful," he said, trying his best to not be overly excited when what he really wanted to do was pull her into his arms and kiss her like the starving man she saw before him. He held back knowing it must have taken a lot for her to call him. He would let her control the direction of the evening.

"Hello. Come on in."

As Kimara opened the door wider, he entered and waited for her to lock the door looking around at the exquisite décor.

"Your place is very nice. The bright colors match your personality.

"Thank you. Did you have any problem finding the place?" she asked.

"None at all. I know this area. In fact, I looked at a condo a few blocks away about a year or two ago. I was thinking about moving and then I changed my mind. It was a moment of weakness since my bank dealt with the financing, I was able to get a first look at the new units and I fell in love with them. Then reality set in and I wanted to be sure where we live is someplace that Journee would flourish and instead, I had some work done to my backyard and had a small playground installed including a covered porch area, a pool and a life-size doll house slash castle. When the weather is warm, I have a hard time getting her out of it," he laughed.

"Condos are nice and convenient and because I'm on the top floor, mine has two levels which I love. It has the feel of a house, but not all the work of one. I'm sure the backyard is a hit with your daughter. How is she?"

Brody liked her attempt at idle chatter. He needed her to find her way to him if they were going to work. This was all about her and what she needed to do to get where he was when it came to their involvement.

"She's good. She's excited about her school trip tomorrow that my mother is chaperoning. She was happy that I came back from vacation, especially after she saw the big bag of gifts I brought home with me," he said.

"I'm glad you were able to get your shopping in before you left. I know you still had that to do."

"I had to fill the rest of my time somehow after you left. Besides, she was promised lots of gifts if she behaved while I was gone. She promised me she was good the whole time."

Kimara was enjoying their conversation, but her body was screaming out loud for him. Yes, she'd missed talking to him, seeing that smile and walking hand in hand with him on the beach. She also missed the closeness she felt when he cradled her in his strong embrace. She couldn't stop thinking about the fierceness and intensity behind his lovemaking. She wanted to talk about their time apart and the struggles she had trying to forget about him when she knew she never would, but right now, she was focused on his handsome face and how much she missed seeing it, touching it and kissing it.

The air between them was growing thick with need and desire – no doubt something both of them noticed. His eyes locked on hers and her eyes locked on him as they each tried to find something to say to lighten the moment, but is that what she really wanted? No, it wasn't, but she couldn't just tell him to get naked because life had stopped for her the moment she left him on that island. Maybe a cooling off period would help, she thought.

"Would you like something to drink? I have wine, beer, water if you choose?" she offered.

"No."

Kimara expected more, but he wasn't making it easy.

"Have you eaten? I can whip up something quick," she offered as her pulse quickened and she tried unsuccessfully to stop picturing him in the throes of passion with her.

"Food is not what I hunger for right at this moment. Do you have any idea how much I've thought about you and how much I've missed you? Did I scare you when I said I loved you? I know you heard it even though we didn't talk about it."

"Yes, it did scare me a little which is why I pushed it to the back of my mind and never brought it up. I've never met anyone and fallen for them as hard as I have fallen for you and when you said that, the only thing I could think about was that was supposed to be about our time on the island and that was it. It wasn't supposed to be about falling in love, but that's exactly what happened. I was scared because I felt the same way, only I wasn't honest enough to say it and see where life could take us. I was a coward," she admitted.

"We're here now."

"I know and for that, I'm glad. One of the happiest days of

my life was the day I got those flowers. I'm grateful that you didn't give up on what we started on the island. The minute I landed here at home, nothing else has been able to keep my focus because the only thoughts I had were of you. Falling in love that fast has never happened to me before and I was married. What does that say?" she asked, not really expecting Brody to answer, but more of a question for herself.

"That says you're letting your heart show you that it's okay to fall in love again even when it's love at first sight. It does exist and I'm glad about that because I'm standing here with you right now and all I want to do is hold you in my arms and make love to you until I pass out. I've missed you and I meant it when I said I loved you. For me, you were love at first sight. I love you," Brody said.

Kimara smiled as her heart began to beat a faster than she ever knew it could. This man standing in front of her putting his heart on his sleeve is why she had also fallen in love at first sight.

"I love you, too and not because you said it, but because it's what's in my heart. You amaze me and I'm lucky that we met and that I had the chance to fall in love with you," Kimara said.

"I'm glad you're no longer running from love."

"I'm sorry for the weeks apart. It's my fault."

"I'm not worried about fault. I'm here, you're here and that's all that matters."

Kimara nodded in agreement.

"Are you sure I can't get you something to drink?" she asked.

"Later. Right now, you wanted to see me, I wanted to see you and my body and mind have been craving you since you left me on the island. I want to feed that hunger right now," Brody admitted and moved closer to her until there was barely any room between them.

Kimara smiled with glee.

"Oh, yes!" she agreed.

Brody's heart beamed as his mind turned to how he wanted all of her, but first he needed to reconnect with lips that drove him wild and kept him away at nights thinking about kissing them again. As their faces came closer and closer together, he reached up with his hand and ran the pad of his thumb along the seam of Kimara's lips, not looking away from her eyes for even a second. He wanted her to remember the look he knew she could see in his eyes that relayed how much he wanted her; how much he loved her. He spoke extremely close to her lips.

"Can you see me? Can you really see me?" he whispered.

Kimara couldn't speak because of the force of the passion that stared back at her. This is why she couldn't walk away from Brody. Everything that he wanted her to know was found in his eyes. She saw the love and felt the thirst and knew that with him was where she needed to be.

Without the use of words, Brody leaned down and kiss her full on the lips while reaching down to pull her arms up and around his neck. He wanted and needed the closeness that fueled his savored want. The moment their lips touched, he was on fire and used that feeling to deepen not just the kiss, but his feelings for her. He knew there was no turning back now.

Kimara felt a heated rush flow through every fiber of her being as Brody's kiss took her to height after tantalizing height where she never wanted to come down from again.

Their lips caressed as she closed her eyes and sighed before joining him in the zealous encounter. Nothing mattered except the feel of his lips on hers again and where her hands rested on his shoulders, she grasped as much of his shirt as she could and held him in place, not wanted him to move even an inch away from her. With this kiss, they were one.

As the kiss ended and she leaned back, the magnitude of her feelings for Brody was now front and center. No more questioning herself or what she was feeling for him. There was also a new, wicked feel to Brody's smile and she was intrigued.

"Tell me, how tame do you think lovemaking should be?" Brody asked. He needed to know because his desire for Kimara was even more powerful than it had been when they were on the island. He felt like a wild animal in heat and the only way to cool his rising temperature was to not only get inside of her, but to be able to pour his passion for her out like a tidal wave.

Tame? Kimara was breathless. The kissing had taken a lot out of her but had also given her the enthusiasm as if she was ready to run a marathon. Tame was the last thing she wanted now that she was in his arms again and on fire. She didn't want soft or fluff, she wanted him in his rarest of forms because she came ready to hold nothing back. She was a woman in love and there was no such thing to her as being tame.

"Don't even think about trying to be tame with me. I'm not fragile and I won't break. We're here because I love you and I want all of you from tame to wild. Whatever you do, just love me," she pleaded and before he could respond, she reached behind his head to his neck and pull him to her. Without any pretense, she kissed him and it wasn't a soft, hello, how are you kind of kiss. It was a I haven't been able to think about anything but you and these lips for weeks and now that I'm encountering them again, I want, no I need my fill, kind of kiss.

Kimara could tell she'd caught Brody off guard because the wildness of the kiss lacked all control and like her, he didn't hold back either. She opened her mouth and in a split second, Brody's tongue was there caressing and pleading with her for more. She gave more and rejoiced when he gave her more as their heads turned from side to side as they tried to meld their mouths even closer together.

The moaning in the air was the only sound heard in the room and when she started to delight in his sounds of pleasure, she realized her moans were even louder than his.

As Brody pulled away too soon, Kimara knew her face showed a frown as Brody laughed.

"Well, I guess I got my answer in words and in that kiss. Now, don't fret sweetheart. I see a disappointing look on your face when I pulled away, but that was because I can't continue to stand here without getting every stitch of those clothes off of you."

Kimara giggled the moment Brody reached for the hem of her thin yellow top. As he pulled it off, she reached for the snap on his jeans, unable to wait another minute before feeling the weight of him in her hands again. Her dreams at night had been filled with him and the emptiness she felt when she woke and discover he wasn't actually there stayed with her all day. Now that she was with him, she wanted to touch and feel every part of him. How could she have ever thought that she would be able to have a casual fling with a man as incredible as Brody. Some women go an entire lifetime not having a man treat her like a queen and she was prepared to leave that feeling behind. Thankfully, she had come to her senses.

Now that her top was off and Brody leaned down to hold each leg up as he pulled her pants down and discarded them along with her heels, she knew this wasn't another dream. She was right where she wanted and needed to be.

"Goodness," Brody exclaimed. Do you wear these sexy matching panties and bra like this all the time? This yellow against your skin is amazing. Have I told you how much I love sexy undies?" Brody asked with a heightened sexiness to his tone.

Kimara beamed while removing his clothes as he spoke.

"What, you thought that was only for the island? Stick with me lover boy and I will show you how sexy my collection really is," she snickered.

"I can't wait. For now, as much as I love this, it has to come off."

Kimara looked at him sideways as if to say he didn't even have to say it. She wanted them both naked and knowing how voracious his appetite was, she was well rested and ready for an all-night love session. She was the cause for them being a part and they had time to make up for.

In the haze of needing him badly, she almost forgot to take the time to again admire his magnificent physique. He stood before her in nothing but black boxer briefs and her breath seemed to catch in her throat when she noticed his erection straining against the fabric. The large mushroom head of him had already pushed up over the top. She smiled remembering the size of him, knowing those briefs wouldn't contain him.

When Brody tilted her head up for another fiery kiss, she reached for his hardness and stroked the tip, reacquainting herself with the strong, powerful feel of him. She rubbed and caressed him even as his mouth trailed from her lips and down around her neck while his wandering hands with those magical fingers hooked into the thin strip of her silky yellow thong, sliding it gently down her legs.

"I have missed you," she uttered trying to do everything she could to distract herself from the fact that her body was already on the brink of a powerful explosion and he hadn't even touch her sweet spot yet.

"I'm glad you did instead of continuing to make us both live in misery. Better late than not at all is the saying, right?".

Kimara was surprised when Brody swiftly picked her up and wrapped her legs around his waist. The immediate contact with his erection against her womanhood had her gyrating her hips in an uncontrollable fashion. She was hot like fire. When he turned with her in his arms, again wildly kissing her, she was happy he was finally making his way to the stairs.

"Never again in misery," she declared loudly. " Right now, a bed is the priority," she added between kisses.

"Oh, we will get there, but right now, I'm not sure I can wait to find a bed to get a taste of you. I promise, we will make our way to a bed before the night is over."

Kimara saw the sky look in Brody's eyes.

"What do you have rolling around in that head of yours?" She asked, knowing she was more than ready to find out.

Without using words, Brody leaned Kimara down on the dark blue carpeted steps, spreading her legs wide and stooping down between them. Kimora's breath was coming out in short, excited breaths at the thought of what she knew was coming next. Their eyes locked as he raised her legs up and over his shoulders. Kimara planted her hands on the steps to brace herself for the impact. Nothing could ever prepare her for what was to come the moment she watched his head move down between her legs.

"You're already glistening and dripping wet for me," he said.

She wanted to respond, but couldn't when the lights appear to have gone out and the visual turned into a fiery sky of rockets and explosions.

Brody's tongue swiped up and then down against her soft folds and the room began to spin. The most delicious and delightful feeling she'd ever experienced hit her as his tongue made sweet delicious love to her. Without thought, her hips began to move and her hands that were braced on the steps, reached in front of her and held on to his head. In her haze, she could see his head moving in a circular motion as he lapped at her, tasting her like a starving man and prayed that the visual of him along with the feeling of his strong, alluring tongue wouldn't take her over the edge too soon. This is what she had been longing for and she wanted it to last.

"I can't hold on much longer," she uttered.

"Don't hold on, baby. I want every drop and we have all night to do this again and again. I want to see you come apart," Brody said.

He lowered his head again and this time, he applied the right amount of pressure he knew she loved and wanting to feel more of her, he reached up and slid his hands up and covered her large breasts with their hard nipples in his hardening under his touch. While his mouth went to work, his hands pinched the hard tips as he rolled them between his fingers. No way was he ever going to get enough of her.

"Brody!" Kimara screamed as her body rose higher and higher until she couldn't hold out any longer. Between his mouth and his hands, the dual ministration was more than any woman could handle and her body gave in to the pleasure as a powerful orgasm slammed into her body while her head thrashed about from one side to the other.

Brody's body was on high alert and ready for more, but nothing could tear him away from the sight of watching Kimara soar high, getting everything she needed from the precise attention he paid to her most intimate place. He wanted to be addicted to the taste of her and wanted her to never forget how good they are together and not just when they made love. He knew immediately upon meeting her that she was much more.

The minute Kimara's body relaxed back into the step, Brody lifted his head and placed kisses around her face.

"Now, I need a bed," he said and lifted her into his arms. Turning away from the steps, he reached for his pants and withdrew the box of condoms he stopped to purchase on his way to her house.

"That was amazing," Kimara said the moment she was able to speak.

"The night is still young, baby. Which way to your bedroom?" he asked as he climbed the steps.

"The large double doors," Kimara said and with amazing anticipation, she was never happier to be heading through those doors and in Brody's arms.

Chapter 21

Now, inside of her bedroom, Brody placed Kimara on her feet once he reached the side of her bed.

"Shall we divest you of these boxer briefs?" she asked.

"No pretense. I like that and absolutely," he grinned.

Kimara looked down before she reached down and again marveled at how virile he looked standing before her long and powerfully aroused. Carefully, she grasped the slides of the garment and slid them down his muscled thighs until they rested at his feet. As she stood back up, she took him into her hands and stroked him from tip to base and admired his reaction to her touch by getting even longer and thicker.

Her body tingled at the thought of the pleasure she knew feeling all of him inside of her could bring. Before Brody could resist, she leaned down and licked the tip of him before taking the head of him into her mouth, lavishing him with an intimate kiss meant to show him the same kind of pleasure he'd shown her on the steps. Kimara delighted in the amount of joy she derived from giving him this kind of pleasure. Adding the stroke of her hand to pleasing him, she could feel his body stiffen as he tried to hold off on reaching completion too soon. She loved the feel and the taste of him and even more, the sounds he was making as she loved him increased her own drive for him. This was her Brody and the more of him that she tried to take in, the louder his moans became until she felt his hands pull her up to her full height.

Brody kissed her deeply on the lips.

"I love the way you make me feel, but in the next second, I need to be inside of you."

Kimara didn't respond. Her answer was in the way she climbed up on her bed like a slick black panther and then turned so that they were facing each other with him still standing and her naked on the bed looking like a wicked she-devil in heat.

"I'm ready," she said on a whisper.

Opening the box of condoms he'd pulled from his pants pocket, Brody quickly opened it, put it on and joined her on the bed by climbing right in between her waiting legs.

"I've missed you," he said again and knew that he would continue to say it until the weight of how much he cared for her sunk in.

"And I love you," Kimara said. "I'm glad you're here," she said and laid back until her body rested on the plush down comforter that covered her bed. She opened her arms and welcomed Brody as he wasted no time sliding between her legs and in between her waiting, wet folds.

"Wild?" he whispered into her ear as his head rested between her shoulder and her head.

"Yes," Kimara replied breathlessly.

Reaching down, Brody gathered each of Kimara's legs into his arms and raised them high so that they could both get the most out of his penetrating strokes. With her legs braced in the fold of his elbows, Brody, on a powerful stroke, surged into her body, not fully on the first stroke. After feeling how wet she still was, he withdrew and this time, surged in until all of him was inside. He moaned, she groaned and they moved together in a rhythm he'd set.

"Hold on tight, baby," he said.

True to what he said, he rocked into her and when she encouraged him to give her more and more, he obliged taking them on a wild ride of sated gratification. A sexual hunger ripped into him like never before and as Kimara ground her hips matching him stroke for stroke, he knew they were both getting close.

Brody lifted his head and captured her gaze the moment she screamed his name.

Kimara's body was on fire and she couldn't seem to get enough of Brody. Feeling him fill her completely her body burned with a need to let the orgasm have its will. She screamed louder when the explosiveness of the impact amazed not just her body, but her mind. The feeling started at her feet and then spiraled through her entire body. She writhed under him taking every stroke into her body with sheer delight. She cried out his name again and again as her orgasm seemed to go on and on taking her higher. She held tightly to Brody's shoulders as he rode her into a frenzy. She wanted to be as close to him as she could get as they experienced ecstasy together.

"So damn hot!" Brody hollered through hard, powerful strokes the moment he felt his orgasm slam into him. He felt wild and crazed as his body, with a mind of its own plunged into her. He continued to dive inside of her with one smooth, deep penetrating stroke after the other until they screamed in sync and in pure satiated ecstasy.

As his body calmed and Kimara's grinds became less intense, Brody released her legs and rubbed them where her legs met her hips, knowing that was where she would have felt the most pressure from the wide-open position he had her in.

Kimara could feel the sweat from Brody's brow as it ran down and dripped on her body when he lifted his head to look into her eyes. She reached up and wiped it away and placed soft kisses along his jaw and whatever part of his face her lips could reach.

"Am I still breathing?" she asked. "I feel like the whole room was shaking and not just the bed. I'm glad it was able to remain standing after that. You were right when you said wild," she said.

"Was I too much? Too hard? I just wanted you with a fierceness. I needed you," he said.

"No, baby, making love to you like this and in any kind of what is what I needed from you."

Brody focused on getting his breathing under control as he could once again focus after the blinding orgasm that zapped everything out of him.

"That was amazing. You are amazing," he said attempting to move to take his weight off of her body.

"No, don't move. I love the feel of you inside of me," she said and held him in place with her legs.

"I'm heavy, baby," Brody said and leaned up to kiss her lips again.

"I love it and you're not too heavy."

"Did I mention how happy I was that you called me?" he asked.

"You did and believe me, you aren't happier than me. Being apart from you was hard and my sister called me on my foolishness."

"Your sister? What did she say?" he said.

This time Brody did move to the side and pulled Kimara with him until she was now on top of him. This allowed him to delight in having her breasts closer to his mouth for him to taste while they talked. Swirling the nipple around in his mouth, he moved his head from one to the other.

"Brody, what are you doing to me? I can't talk while you're doing that."

Brody giggled, but didn't stop.

"You're the one laying on me all naked and stuff and you want me to just lay here and not take advantage of this vantage position I have. I will try, but I won't commit to that try," he laughed.

Kimara laughed, too.

"Okay, if your try is all I can get. I already forgot what I was supposed to be saying," she said. Kimara was trying her best to focus on her thoughts and not on Brody's delicious mouth and tongue.

"Your sister," he said.

"Okay, I can't think about my sister with my breasts in your mouth."

Brody's whole body rocked with laughter.

"Point taken," he said and paid attention.

"Okay, I told my sister that I felt empty now that I was back to reality. I didn't tell her everything about you, but I told her that I'd met you and that it was my idea to leave what we had on the island. What stunned her was my admission that in hindsight, it had been one of the worse decisions of my life. Since that day, every time she sees me, she would shake her head at me for not allowing myself to love you the way I really wanted to because I was holding on to something in the past."

"You were?"

"I was and I felt like I wasn't deserving of the kind of happiness I felt being with you. I wasn't sure enough time had passed for me to be that happy."

"Baby, you know that's not true. You can't help when you fall in love. We both suffered a loss and that we will never forget, but we're also entitled to have love again. In a few short days, we found that love and it wasn't meant to stay on that island. I want to date you, love you and see what we can make together," he said.

"You were surer of us than I was." Kimara felt bad about that. How could she not feel as sure about them as he had? They were having the same feelings on the island, yet she was willing to walk away. She didn't deserve a man as great as him.

"I want you to know that even though I pulled back and didn't pursue you, I had no plans of just letting go. I wanted to give you the time that you needed to know that we were meant for each other. I knew that if you missed me half as much as I missed you, only time was in the way of our being together. I was willing to wait as long as needed for you."

"Were you? What if I never came around?" Kimara asked. The thought that it could have been a real situation had fear invade her heart. She never wanted to go back to the few weeks apart that they had. She could see them dating now that they were back to reality and she wanted to be all in.

"Yes, baby, I was. The time we spent together on that

island wasn't something casual though we wanted to convince ourselves that's what it was. The heart knows and that's what mattered. Now, that is in the past and here we are. I have no plans of letting you out of my life again, so get used to seeing me," Brody explained.

Kimara looked from his face down to that part of him that was already growing hard and strong between them.

"I could definitely get used to seeing you, especially like this," she said and leaned down to kiss him. "My body is already stirring with need for you again. Is that crazy?" she asked.

"Can you feel me? That's not crazy at all."

"I want to be wild with you all night long," Kimara admitted.

Brody leaned close to her ear.

"Show me," he whispered.

Kimara couldn't wait to show him that he wasn't the only one who could be wild!

Chapter 22

"Daddy? Where's Nana?"

Brody smiled at Journee's look of amazement that she woke up from her nap and he was who she saw. She had spent Friday night at his parent's house and he showed up this morning just as his mother said Journee had fallen asleep while watching her favorite cartoon. Without waking her, he put her in the car and drove home and prepared for a fund day at the local carnival. Today was also the day he was planning on introducing Journee to Kimara.

After their first night back together two weeks ago, he and Kimara had been dating, yet not around Journee. They agreed to see how things were going and then he would ease Journee into the idea that he was seeing someone. On nights where his parents or sister had Journee, he spent the night at her place. Now was the time for his two loves to meet.

"Nana is at home. Nana and Grampy are taking the day to go out and have some fun and it looks like you're stuck with me. Is that alright?" he asked, smiling.

Brody got his answer when Journee wrapped her arms around his neck and held on for dear life.

"No work today?" she asked.

"No work today. You and I are going to have a special day today," he said laying out clothes for Journee to change into.

"I love pink, daddy," she said when she saw him getting her favorite outfit from her closet.

"I know you do and I love seeing you in pink. Let's get you washed up and into some clean clothes."

Brody reached down and lifted Journee into his arms as they headed into the bathroom.

"Pumpkin, remember daddy told you about a lady that he really likes?"

Journee nodded her head.

"Well, I want you to meet her today. We're going to a carnival to have some fun."

Journee started bouncing up and down.

"A carnival? Can I ride the rides and get some popcorn?" she asked.

"Yes, you can."

"Daddy, do you love this lady?" she asked as he wiped her face.

"Yes, daddy does love her. Is that okay?" he asked.

Over the past few weeks, he and Kimara had fallen into a routine that was as comfortable as breathing. She admitted as he had, that their lives finally felt like they were back on track. It was natural for him to call or text her in the morning to wish her a wonderful day and then later that evening, he looked forward to her call where she shared her day and he shared his. It was during one of their talks that he let her know of his plan to introduce her to Journee. He thought it would be a great idea for them to spend the day doing something fun, so that the whole focus was not on them meeting, but on the three of them having a fun day. He was happy that Kimara was just as excited as he was.

They had made plans to meet at the carnival and then perhaps after, they would go to Journee's favorite pizza place to top off their day. He was looking forward to spending the day with his two favorite girls.

"Yes, that's okay. Is she really pretty?" Journee asked as he ran water for her to take a bath.

"She is beautiful and you're going to like her."

"Does she have a little girl like me?" she asked.

"No, she doesn't have any children."

"What's her name?"

Brody knew Journee would have lots of questions and he was ready for them.

"Her name is Ms. Kimara."

"Does she like little girls like me?"

"She loves little girls like you and she can't wait to meet you. She's been talking about it all week. Now, I'm going downstairs while you get a bath and put on the clothes on your bed and then we can head out and meet Ms. Kimara."

"How did I get home daddy? I was at Nana and Grampy's house."

"I picked you up. I decided not to go to work today and instead spend the day with my two favorite girls, you and Ms. Kimara. We're going to have a lot of fun, right?" he asked.

"Daddy? Would my mommy like Ms. Kimara?"

Brody stood stunned for a minute. It wasn't too often that Journee brought up Peyton. He'd told her about Peyton as soon as he thought she was ready to handle the reason why she didn't have her mommy with her every day. He kept pictures of Peyton in Journee's room and he knew that she loved the book of photos he made for her of pictures of Peyton and the only one he had that was taken of Peyton with Journee resting on her right before she passed away. It was important that Journee knew how much Peyton had been looking forward to being her mother.

"I think your mommy would like Ms. Kimara. She would be happy that daddy found someone to love. Daddy's love for mommy was so great that for a long time, he wasn't sure he would ever find someone to love again. Ms. Kimara makes daddy very happy."

"I know. I like it when you smile."

"You know that daddy will always love you first, right? You are everything in this world to me and you always will be. Ms. Kimara is a friend coming into our lives and is looking forward to spending time with you and daddy. Is that okay?" he asked.

"Yes. If you like her then I do, too."

Brody smiled at his big girl.

"Now, take your bath, put your shorts and shirt on and daddy will get your sneakers and meet you downstairs."

Turning, Brody left her room after grabbing her shoes and went to his own room. He'd cleaned up earlier, hoping he could convince Kimara to spend the evening at his house. They were growing closer and closer with each day. He never thought he'd feel as deeply for a woman again the way he now felt for Kimara. He loved the sound of her voice and earlier in the week, he'd taken off early from work as she did and they spent the afternoon at her house watching a movie and eating greasy pizza until it was time for him to pick Journee up from school. They were finding even more in common and they even spent some time talking about the past and what happened to both of them five years ago.

As he left his room and headed downstairs to wait for Journee, he recalled that conversation with Kimara where they decided to finally share the events of five years ago and once and fall, put it behind them and move on together.

His sister had taken Journee with her for a spa day and with a few hours after work until she brought Journee back, he spent time with Kimara at her house on a day when she worked from home in the morning and had the afternoon free. Somehow, they got on the topic of the train crash and Kimara mentioned it was thoughts of Ellis that made her question her feelings for him. She hadn't been sure it was time for her to get involved with a man since in her mind, she was supposed to spend her life with Ellis.

He admitted to having some reservations at first. His life with Peyton had played a role in his inability to commit to any woman after she passed away. He casually dated from one woman to another, but he never let any of them get close until he met Kimara. The pull to her was too strong to avoid and walk away from. They turned their attention away from the television and focused on letting each other talk through the pain of that day in hopes that their future would be free of any reservations about the past. That talk that day was exactly what he needed as he recalled it.

"Other than talking to my family and very close friends, I haven't shared anything about the accident with others, not even the news outlets that hounded me for months and months about doing an interview. I couldn't talk about it then, but I want to talk about it with you," he said.

Kimara leaned back in the chair and gave Brody her full attention.

"Okay, whenever you're ready," she said, making sure she was giving him the comforting voice she knew he would need.

"That morning, Peyton got up extra early, excited about the train ride. She was planning a trip to go visit her family out of town and I was the one who suggested the train because being pregnant, she was tired all of the time and I knew the car ride of several hours may be too much for her. Peyton had been adopted and her family wasn't very large. Her parents were gone having passed a few years before and the rest of the family embraced her. She hadn't see them much and was excited about the trip and how she could relax on the train. I can't tell you how that suggestion I made for her to take the train ate away at me for a long time after the accident."

Kimara reached over and took Brody's hands in hers. She could feel the trembles in them as he continued. What was most important right now was for him to know that she was right here with him for all the support he needed.

"There was no way for you to know what would happen on the train that day," she said.

"I know, but you know how guilt works. When I think back on everything that happened that day, I've had moments of wondering what if," he said.

"I know and if you don't let go of that guilt, it will eat at you forever and even though I had never met Peyton, she would not want that."

"Thank you. Well, she was excited and so was I. We agreed that she would take a few months off from work to prepare for the baby and then she was going to take the first year and possibly more off to stay at home with the *baby because she was really big on the bonding thing. I decided on the train for the trip when what I should have done was taken the time off from work and drove there with her for a short vacation, but I was in the middle of negotiating a major contract with a bank client and so I suggested she go ahead and spend time with her family since she had started getting bored sitting around the house. She called me from the train to tell me that taking it was the best recommendation I'd ever made because she avoided the stress that came with driving long distance and she'd already met a nice woman on the train who was also pregnant and they struck up a conversation and were chatting like old friends. A couple of hours later, I was finally heading into the office when I heard about the train crash and my world fell apart. It took me hours to get any information and when I thought the worse, it was as bad as I had imagined. Peyton was alive, but barely clinging to life. What they found was Journee, whom she still carried was still doing good, but they feared she wasn't ready to be delivered. We agreed to keep Peyton on life support until they knew Journee would survive outside of her body. After that crash, my life turned into an ever-winding rollercoaster ride. Peyton was one of twenty-eight who survived, but severely injured. I will never forget the feeling of dread that came over me when I was told that they couldn't do anything for Peyton and that she would eventually succumb to her injuries. I couldn't think about anything other than I was going to lose Peyton and I didn't get the chance to apologize for her being on that train."*

"Was your family with you? What about her family? I hope you had support as you went through that," Kimara *said and reached over to hold his hands in hers.*

"Peyton's family was great and her cousins rotated coming to help with house stuff and sitting with Peyton to give me a little bit of a break. I didn't want her to be alone, not even for a moment. My parents and sister drove down and took turns staying with us at the hospital. My mom was retired, but my sister had a husband and her own children so she was back and forth for the few weeks that we kept Peyton alive. The moment the doctors thought Journee would survive, they performed a C-section on Peyton and Journee was immediately taken to the neonatal intensive care unit. After stitching Peyton back up, they put her back in her room and then I had to make the decision to remove her from life support. Peyton looked forward to being a mother and because of the crash, she wouldn't get to do that. She wouldn't get to see the beautiful little girl Journee turned out to be. Two days later, I signed the consent form to have her removed from life support. I asked them to briefly bring Journee into the room and lay her on Peyton's chest. I wanted the last heart beat that Peyton heard was that of her own daughter, knowing she was going to be okay. I swear, the moment they placed Journee on her bare chest, Peyton's monitors went crazy. I think she was aware that Journee was there, alive and that she would be okay. We only laid her there for about a minute and the moment we took her away, Peyton slipped away. At that time, I hadn't given the baby a name yet. I came up with it after Peyton died because of the journey she took to get here. It wasn't an easy one and her name was fitting for the situation. I named her Journee Peyton Grey after her mother and as she gets older, I will always remind her of

the incredible woman her mother was."

"What a beautiful name. Peyton would be proud of you and Journee is a blessed little girl."

"I love her with everything in me and she looks more and more like her mother all the time. I've finally come to terms with losing her and my trip to the island was me letting her know that though I will never forget her, it was time I got back on with my life and not dwell on the past so much. There were times when Journee would see me and wonder why I was sad and I needed to stop that. Since I've met you, all I do is smile. She often catches me smiling and asks what's making me smile so hard. My love for her makes me smile every day and now having you in my life I walk around with a permanent smile on my face because I know that being with you is exactly where I'm supposed to be. Now, your turn," Brody said and patiently waited for Kimara to pull the strength she needed to go back to that day five years in the past as he had just done.

Kimara knew that if she was ever going to go back to that day and tell the story, she couldn't think of anyone other than Brody to tell it to.

"Ellis was on his way to a big business meeting. He was about to launch a new marketing firm with a few of his partners and we were preparing to move and he decided to take the train that day so that he could look over his proposal up until the last minute. At the time of the accident, I was in the office when my sister called and asked me if I had heard from Ellis. The way she asked had me on high alert and I knew something was wrong. I remember dialing Ellis' cell phone so many times that my fingers started to feel numb. Each time I got his voicemail and

became more and more frightened. I knew that if he wasn't on that train and he'd heard about the accident, he would have called to let me know that he was okay. After spending hours at the train station waiting for information, my sister and I got in the car and drove to where the accident was. It was a horrible scene from what we could see on the television and once we arrived, we couldn't get anywhere close to it and little information was given out. They finally started calling names and said we should head over to the hospital for more information. That made me hopeful because I figured they wouldn't send us there if he had died. Once there, my sister and I were taken into a private room where they told me that Ellis was among the dead and my world crashed and burned. I heard the doctor say the words, but I couldn't process that they were telling me he had died and it looked like he died instantly. He was in the train car where only ten people out of forty survived and those ten were critically injured. I was numb for a long time trying to think of my world without Ellis in it. Things were happening so fast and television cameras were all in our faces. After a while, my sister convinced me to leave the hospital and we stayed at a local hotel until Ellis' body was released to me. For a long time, I couldn't figure out how I made it from one day to the next," she explained.

"Peyton was in the second car that turned over on its side. I was at the hospital that day and for many more until Journee was finally released which was three months later," Brody added.

Kimara held on to his hands tighter.

"I've never experienced such pain in my life," she said. "I know what you went through. After that, I walked around *numb for months and still years later, I've had struggles getting through. I took that trip because I knew it was time to finally get myself back together. I quit my job and have been doing some side consulting work for the past few years. Sometimes I work out of an office, but I love the time I get to work from home. Ellis and I had big dreams for our lives and once his firm was up and running, we were going to start our family and I was going to do as your wife was planning to do which was stay at home for some years and raise our kids. I'm happy you got to experience fatherhood and keep a piece of Peyton in Journee," she said.*

Brody smiled.

"In some way, I think Peyton and Ellis had a hand in you and I meeting. Imagine how crazy it is that we never connected and we live only miles away, but we go to the same island for some time away at the exact same time and my first night there, I saw you on the beach," he admitted.

"I may have to agree with you on that. The day you arrived, I saw you when you checked in and then that night when we connected at the party, I remembered you from earlier in the day. Perhaps Ellis and Peyton knew that you and I had been hurting long enough and that it was time to let go and find the love again that was waiting for us," Kimara said.

"It was fate baby and I have not been this happy in a very long time. I lost the love of my life once and I never want to go through that ever again. I'm in this with you for the long haul and I hope you are, too," Brody said.

"I am. I love you," Kimara said.

"I love you, too. Whatever had a hand in our meeting has my full gratitude. Now, all I have to do is introduce you to

Journee and the circle is closed. What do you say to spending the day soon with Journee and I at a carnival? I saw some information that one is coming to town and setting up at one of the local farms. They'll be rides, food, fun and games and Journee loves amusement park rides. I'm taking her to Disneyland later this summer because I know how much she loves these things."

"Oh, she will love that and I would love to meet her. The carnival sounds like fun."

Brody leaned forward and kissed her sweetly.

"Thanks for sharing your story with me."

"Thank you for sharing with me. I think it has helped us both move beyond anything from our past that could keep us from freely walking into our future, together."

"Daddy! I'm ready," Journee said coming into the room.

Brody smiled after reminiscing about the talk he and Kimara had and now it was time for them to meet.

"Here, let's get your shoes on and we're ready to go."

"Yeah!" Journee said.

Brody knew her excitement was exactly how he was feeling.

Chapter 23

Kimara walked into the restaurant and looked around for her mother and sister. Her mother had called earlier in the week and suggested they get together since they hadn't seen each over for almost two weeks. In that time, Kimara was getting to know Brody and his beautiful daughter and to her, life couldn't be better. She thought her mother and sister would be upset that every time they called, she was busy either working or out with Brody. She smiled as she made her way through the throngs of tables until she spotted her sister waving wildly at her.

"Hey!" Casey said as soon as she reached the table. After hugging them, Kimara sat down and reached for the menu.

"Uh, I need a glass of wine. I've had the busiest day," she said smiling.

"Uh, sis, you look amazing!" Casey said.

"Yes, she does."

Kimara looked at her mother and winked.

"I take it that smile is permanent. You are glowing."

"Yes, mom, it is permanent and lately all I've been doing is smiling."

She was about to add more, but the waitress showed up to take their orders. The table was already full of appetizers and she wasn't ready to order food yet. After ordering her wine, she turned to Casey.

"So, should I assume that smile has a lot to do with Brody? You've been seeing a lot of each other lately. We've barely seen you or talked to you in a few weeks. I'm not complaining as long as the reason is a happy one and it has to do with that fine man you're seeing," Casey said.

"It does and I couldn't be happier. We have been having a wonderful time and thanks for coming to dinner a few weeks ago and meeting him. When I told him the dinner invite involved you and mom, he was excited and more than ready."

"That was the last time we saw you. I tell you there isn't a more perfect man around. I see why you've fallen in love with him. No one can blame you. Is he that loving and adoring all the time?" Casey asked.

"Yes, he is. You know when you meet someone, you get the person they want you to like, but then after a while the real them comes out? With Brody, who I met is who I'm still with. He makes me so happy," Kimara said as she looked over the menu.

"Well, I am extremely happy for you. I wasn't sure you would ever be this happy again," her mother said.

"I know and I know I made you worry, but I'm okay. In fact, I'm great."

"What have you been doing since we last saw you?" Casey asked.

"I told you about his daughter and the day I spent with them at the carnival. We did talk about that recently. Since that day, Brody and I have been on several dates and just last night we went to a movie. His daughter was with his sister for the night, so we took advantage of his free time. After that we went to a supper club and I met a group of his friends, including his best friend Nelson and his wife. Everyone was nice, cordial and welcoming and thanked me for bringing Brody back to life. Apparently, I wasn't the only one still going through after five years. I'm glad we found each other."

"So are we," her mother said. "It warms my heart to see you this happy."

"You know it feels like a whirlwind romance because it's only been a little over a month, but I feel like I've been dating a best friend I've had my whole life. We talk about everything and we share what we would like our lives to be like in the future. I even told him about my dream of having a farm with animals and a big house with lots of rooms to roam around in. I haven't thought about that in years, but talking with Brody, I think that's what I'm going to do with some of the settlement money I have and never did anything with."

"What about your consultant work here in the city? If you get this farm, it's not going to be close by," Casey said.

"I know and I've thought about that. I can do my consultant work from anywhere as long as I have an internet connection. I want to finally start doing some of the things I've been dreaming about, but haven't done. I feel refreshed, like new life has been breathed into me."

"We can tell. How has Brody's daughter been around you? I know you love kids, but sometimes it can be rough when a child sees another person taking attention away from them," her mother said.

Kimara had gotten nothing but love from Journee.

"It's been great. I found another animal lover in her and whenever I'm around her, we get into a deep discussion about animals and I even told her about the farm I want to have one day. The other night, he invited me over and the three of us ordered pizza delivery, kicked back, watched movies and pigged out on ice cream. We laughed and Journee even read me a book. It was adorable. I love being with them," she said.

"Sounds like a family to me. I'm just saying," Casey said.
"It feels like one, but I don't want to put the cart before the horse. We are enjoying each other and every day, learning more and more about each other."

"Could you see yourself married again? I'm not saying to Brody, though he would be a great catch, I mean married again at all?" Casey asked.

Kimara didn't want to admit that she had been thinking about that. After meeting Brody, she realized she could love again and if she could do that, she could see herself opening up to being married again. She missed that kind of closeness and one day hoped to have it again and in time to have children of her own.

"I can see that and don't be surprised when I say this, but I still want to have children. I know I had given up hope on that when Ellis died, but being around Journee, I realized I was meant to be a mother and love a child or hopefully children."

Kimara looked over as her mother grabbed a tissue and wiped her eyes.

"Kimmy, you made our mother cry," Casey said.

"I'm sorry, mom," she said.

"No, no, don't apologize. These are happy tears. I'm

overwhelmed with joy at seeing you this happy again. You were always meant to be this happy and I'm glad a fantastic man like Brody came into your life. You're living again and that makes me very, very happy."

"Brody does make me happy, but mostly I'm finally realizing life is meant to be lived in the present, not in the past. I almost gave up on what Brody and I have right now. I'm glad he didn't give up on us. The one thing we finally did was sit down and talk through what we had gone through five years ago and the impact it had on our lives. We decided our meeting was meant to be because only someone who had gone through what we did could understand and help each other through. Things between us are so right."

"Well, I'm glad and I hope all this happiness continues. I'm surprised you had time for an early dinner tonight. I thought you were going to cancel," Casey said.

"It was a busy day, but tonight I'm heading over to Brody's house after dinner. He has a business trip coming up in a few days and will be out of town. I'm already missing him."

"Well, then let's order dinner so we can get you out of here and off to your man," her mother said.

"Really mom?" Casey quipped.

"Don't hate."

Kimara broke out in an uncontrollable laugh. She loved time with them, but was looking forward to an evening with her two loves, Brody and Journee.

**

"Daddy, did you know that Ms. Kimara likes animals, too? She likes horses, cows, dogs, pigs and all the animals on a farm."

Brody listened while Journee talked a million miles a

minute.

"Yes, I know and one day, she's going to have her very own farm with lots and lots of animals, he said.

"Can I visit her farm and play with the animals?"

"I'm sure she would like that," he said.

"You can come too, daddy."

Brody laughed heartily.

"Why, thank you for inviting me to come along."

He held up three books for her to choose from. When she pointed to her favorite, he sat on the side of the bed next to her.

"I like Ms. Kimara daddy. She's a lot of fun," Journee said.

"I'm glad you like her. Daddy likes her a lot. Did you have a good time tonight?" he asked as she snuggled up close to him, ready for her story.

"Yes, daddy. Can we do it again? Can we invite Ms. Kimora over again?" Journee asked.

"We can do that all the time. Are you okay if she comes over more often when you're home? I don't want to take any time away from the fun you and daddy have. You have to be okay with that. It's always been you and daddy and no one else and now Ms. Kimora is hanging out with us. You and daddy are a team and we make decisions together. If anything is wrong with this, you tell me, okay?"

Brody had never brought another woman around Journee before. He'd casually dated, but he never saw any of those women as potentials for something more like he saw in Kimara. He saw a future with her every time he looked in her face. They had so much in common and they had great fun when they were together which had nothing to do with intimacy. What they had was much more than that and to show her how serious he was, he couldn't wait to introduce her to Journee and let her know he'd never done that before. They had something very special.

"Nothing wrong, daddy. I like Ms. Kimara a whole lot. I like having her around. We have a lot of fun together at the park, watching movies and eating pizza. Can we do it again tomorrow?"

"Maybe not tomorrow. I'm planning on having more fun things like we did today. Is it okay if Ms. Kimara joins us sometimes?" he asked.

Brody was happy Journee and Kimara hit it off right away. They were his life.

"Yes. Can she come to my birthday party? Auntie Brynne said my party is going to be fun and I can invite my friends. Ms. Kimara is my friend now, too, right daddy?"

Brody kissed the top of her head.

"Yes, she is. Now, let's read this story so you can get some sleep. You've had a busy day."

**

Kimara was wiping down the long gray and black kitchen island when she looked up to see Brody standing in the doorway to the kitchen watching her.

"Hi," she said.

"Hi," he said coming over to her and pulling her into his arms.

"I had fun today with you and Journee. Thanks for inviting me. She in an incredible and bright little girl. Are you sure she's only four about to be five and not older?" she asked and smiled.

"Sometimes I can't tell if I'm running things around here or if she is. You look naturally comfortable here in my house."

"I feel comfortable and I love your house, especially your kitchen. There are chefs who would be amazed by the design."

"I had the entire house overhauled about a year ago. I needed a change. It's definitely beautiful and spacious. One day I hope to have a large house with lots of rooms and lots of land."

"Ah, the farm. You know you should do that right? If you have a dream of something, you shouldn't wait to make it happen for yourself," Brody said and meant it. His dream was to make him, Kimara and Journee a family. It may seem like fast work, but he knew how short life can be and he didn't want to waste any of it.

"You came back down pretty fast. Did you get through the whole book with Journee?" she asked as she put the plates away they'd eaten on.

"I got through about two pages and she was down for the count. I usually can get through a full book, but it's been a long day. Thank you for spending the evening with us. I wasn't sure if I'd get to spend time with you before my business trip."

"How long will you be gone?"

"Just three days."

"I'm going to miss you," Kimara said turning toward him and leaning back against the counter.

"I'm going to miss you, too. I'm happy knowing that you'll be here when I get back. You and I work."

"Yes, we do. If anyone ever asks me if I believe in love at first sight, I know now that it can happen."

"We are the poster children for that," Brody laughed and

came up to her.

Brody took her hand as they walked back into his family room.

"I want to talk to you about something," he said and turned off the television.

"Okay," Kimara said curiously.

"I love you and I love being with you. I know we didn't expect to fall in love and be in love after only one day of meeting. It happened and I haven't been this happy in a long time. It's because of you. I don't know how you feel about what the future holds, but I want mine to be me, you and Journee. I want to love you close up and personal. I want to come home to you every day and be the family that we already are. What I'm saying is, I want to marry you. I know you are probably saying you may believe in love at first sight, but marriage after two months is a bit much and I agree. What I'm saying is, I want to ask you to marry me and work towards that. We can get married whenever you're ready, if you want that too, but I want you to know that when I met you, you were it for me. I knew it then and I know it now. Seeing you with Journee and the life we are living together is the kind of love I want to have forever."

Kimara sat stunned. Brody had just asked her to marry him and she couldn't stop how fast her heart was racing. They had both been through a lot and he was right that life was too short to question happiness. They had found it and she wouldn't want any life that didn't include him and Journee.

"I'm ready, Brody. I'm ready and I don't want to wait. We know how life can go and how it can change with the blink of an eye. I want a life with you and Journee. I love you so much and I love that little girl upstairs. The day we met it was meant to be and our being here now with you asking me to marry you was meant to be, too. I don't need to wait and I don't have to think too hard about it. I love you and I would marry you today, tomorrow or any other day."

Brody reached into this pocket for a gift he'd been holding on to for the past week. He had taken his sister with him to purchase the perfect ring. When he called and told Brynne that he was planning to propose to Kimara, she didn't hesitate to show her excitement. She knew what he had gone through and knew that a happy life waits for no one. She'd told him if Kimara made him happy and Journee loved he, she was happy for him and wanted to be a part by going with him to pick out a beautiful ring.

Pulling out a navy blue velvet ring box, Brody slid from the chair down to one knee and looked Kimara in the eyes. He smiled when he saw a single tear slide down her face knowing it was a sign that she was as happy as he was. He opened the box, showing her what was inside. Taking the ring out, he placed it on her finger.

"I love you, baby. Thank you for coming into my life," he said.

Kimara wiped away the tears that fell to her cheeks and looked from the ring to Brody.

"I love you, too. I look forward to being your wife," she said and went into his arms.

"No more than me, sweetheart."

They sat like that for a few minutes before Kimara finally leaned back.

"What about Journee? Does she know?"

"I haven't told her. I plan to tell her in the morning and I want you there with me when I tell her. Are you ready for that?"

Kimara was nervous. She had developed a great friendship with Journee and wanted nothing more than to be her second mommy, never wanting to take Peyton's place, but to finish the work of mom that Peyton was unable to complete.

"Yes, I am. If I'm not, I need to be," she said.

"Journee loves you. Tonight, she actually invited me to visit your farm with her when you get it and we will be getting that farm."

"And babies?" Kimara asked. She wanted babies.

"As many babies as we can possibly think to have. We both know how fragile life can be and I don't want to waste any of it. Journee will be excited about one day being a big sister. Between that and the farm of animals, I'd say Journee is on board," he laughed.

Kimara laughed, too.

"This ring is beautiful. When did you get it?" she asked.

"My sister went out with me about a week ago to get it. I was nervous about what to get. She was excited about it and wanted to be a part of it. You won her over the first time she met you and when I told her I wanted to propose, she told me it was about time."

"Brynne has become like a second sister. She and Casey are going to have a blast getting to know each other. We're going to be family," she said.

"Yes, we are. That will be another happy day. Can I convince you to spend the night with me?"

"Spending the night? What about Journee?"

"She'll be out until at least seven in the morning and I want to tell her first thing in the morning. I want you there.

She'll need to get used to you living under the same roof with us when we get married. Tonight, I want you in my arms," he said.

"Are you sure? It won't be too much too soon for her to see me here in the morning?" she asked.

"Baby, I'm living in each day like it's our last and for me, us being a family starts now. I love you," he said again.

"Okay, well no lovemaking. You know how loud you can be," she said, laughing.

Brody laughed loud, too.

"I promise to make love to you quietly if you can control how you like to scream my name," he quipped.

Kimara fake punched him in the shoulder and Brody laughed even harder.

"You scream my name as much as I scream yours," she countered.

"I look forward to screaming it for many, many years to come.

<u>Epilogue</u>
One years later

"So, is this the house?" Brody asked.

Kimara couldn't believe her eyes. She looked across the sprawling eighty acres of land, or as much of it as she could see from her vantage point. Everything about it so far was exactly like she dreamed it would be. There was a large main family house that sat in the middle of the large estate with a large porch that wrapped around the entire house. There were two levels and according to the paperwork, the house boasted six bedrooms, eight baths and more space than she ever could have imagined. She smiled no one else in the world could be as happy as she was at this minute.

After a whirlwind engagement, three months later, she and Brody were married in a ceremony with both of their families and friends in attendance. She wore a winter white gown while Brody wore a gray tuxedo that matched the one his best friend and best man, Nelson wore. Her sister stood as her matron of honor while Journee served as flower girl in the same color dress as her gown.

After they shared with Journee that they were getting married, she couldn't have been happier. They let her be a part of all of the wedding planning and she even loved helping Kimara pack up her house to move in with them. For the past year, they lived as a happy family.

Today, Brody was making sure a dream of hers came true. He had searched for and found the perfect farm for her. Today, he brought her out to see if and if it passed her test, they were signing the papers later in the day to purchase it. Kimara looked around and saw everything as if Brody had been a front seat driver to her dream.

There were several barns which was plenty of space for all of the animals she wanted to raise. She could imagine lots of horses finding a home on the land. No longer doing consultant work, she would be able to give all of her attention to turning the farm into a home for them all. She was most happy about all of the extra space the house would have. She wanted both of their families to be able to come out and have their own space at the house whenever they visited. The way their family had expanded since the wedding was only the beginning. In four months, their family would be increasing by two with the birth of their twins.

Kimara and Brody had been happy and shocked the day her doctor told them that she was not only pregnant, but was pregnant with twins, something that ran on Brody's side of the family. He was a twin, so it could have happened with them.

Her life was coming full circle and she never thought she would be this happy ever again.

"Well, what do you think?" Brody asked.

"I love it, daddy!" Journee chimed in.

"I love it too!" Kimara said.

"What will my room look like?" Journee said.

"You and I can do whatever you want with your room. I'm going to have a lady friend of mine come over before we move in and help us pick out everything."

"I want a princess room. Can I have that?" she asked.

"You can have whatever you want," Brody said.

"So, this is it then?" Kimara asked.

"All I needed was your okay and it's ours."

Kimara couldn't wait. They had taken the money they each received from the settlement after the accident and planned out the life of their dreams starting with the new house. Second, Brody wanted her to focus on family and not on working since money was not an issue for them. She couldn't be happier knowing that she could focus on her family and her farm. Journee had received a separate settlement and they agreed to put that money aside to allow her to do whatever she wanted with it when she turned twenty-one.

"You have my okay on everything. Thank you for being everything I could want," Kimara said rubbing her expanding belly.

"Thank you for being my love at first sight."

Enjoy this excerpt from *"My First Love"* – another romance novel from Cheryl Barton

Who ever thought a father would ruin his son's life for the sake of a basketball career? Ethan didn't and he wondered how he would ever forgive his father for what he'd done when it came to his first love.

Moriah Bennett loved the Miami, Florida heat and today, she had a feeling the ninety-five-degree heat was having a dire effect on her husband's ability to use common sense in his decision making.

"It's for his own good," she heard Tellis say.

She stared in amazement as her husband of over twenty years attempted to defend the rationale behind the poor choice he made when he involved himself in their son's personal life. His nonchalant arrogance was rubbing her the wrong way. "Is it for his own good or for your own good?" she asked, annoyed. "You can't control every aspect of our children's lives, especially Ethan. He loves that girl and nothing you do is ever going to change that."

Moriah knew she was talking to a man who wasn't paying her any attention. After many years of marriage, she could read the signs.

Tellis Bennett was the love of her life, but right now, she didn't recognize the man she fell in love with at a young age, married and raised three children with. He was one of the top players in the national basketball league and a man used to having his way and having people under his control. To him, there was no exception to that when it came to his children. Though she disagreed with his latest actions that could possibly scar their son for life, she knew he loved

Ethan and wanted the best for him, but she had a feeling what he'd done wasn't for Ethan's best interest, but for his own.

Ethan was their oldest child at eighteen, Eli their youngest at fourteen and Esha, their beautiful daughter, who at sixteen had recently won Miss Teen Florida. To Moriah, her life was her husband and children and even though they lived a life of luxury as a result of her husband's career, they remained humble, not flaunting their wealth while still living in a manner that showed their appreciation for what they were blessed with.

As Tellis' partner in love and in life, they reminded their children of the importance of an education and being thankful for every opportunity afforded them. She and Tellis were able to provide top-notch education that she hoped would show them that there was more to life than money. She wanted to see them come into their own, making decisions that made them happy in love and in life. Her husband, on the other hand, frustrated her with his need to guide every aspect of their lives, giving their children no freedom in the choices they made. She knew that he had a way of making them think that their decisions were theirs when in fact, he used persuasion to make them see things his way. That worked on Eli and Esha, but not so much on Ethan. With him, Tellis had to find another way to make him see things his father's way. His latest antics, she knew, would be one of the biggest mistakes of his life and she had a feeling they were going to live to regret it.

"Moriah, Ethan has no idea what it means to really be in love. That boy is in lust with a girl over her cute face and body that send his hormones into the stratosphere like every other teenage boy his age. The head he's thinking with could ruin any chance he'll have at a successful career and life," he explained. Tellis was disturbed by the fact that Moriah was fighting him and not going along like she typically did. "That girl will have him locked down with a million kids, leaving him struggling to get by because if he stays with her, they won't be living off of my money. I had her family looked into and her mother can't even keep up with the number of kids she's already popped out and her father is a rolling stone. She doesn't have much of an example when it comes to life's successes and I want more for my son than some young girl who sees the way to success is in between her legs."

Fire brimmed in Moriah as she used her eyes to throw invisible daggers at Tellis. She didn't recognize the man she loved and married. She'd seen him angry over the years, but the words coming out of his mouth were vile and hateful. She did agree that Ethan and Valencia were a little too close for her comfort at their age, but talking down to a young girl they still didn't know a lot about wasn't the answer. Who her parents are didn't provide evidence that she'd be the same way. She preferred talking to their son to be sure he wasn't on the path to make a mistake that could cost him more than he could imagine. If by chance Ethan and Valencia were having sex at their age, she knew that Tellis had talked to him and Eli about responsibility and safety when it came to sexual activity and she knew Ethan wouldn't make a mistake like that. She didn't want to know what her son did in his private time, she only wanted him to be happy, not take risks and be respectful of any girl he decided to get involved with. She wanted all of her kids to find happy, loving relationships like she had with Tellis. What she didn't want was for her husband to lay the ground work for deceit in the name of looking out for their best interests. What he was doing to Ethan was wrong and the choices he made, right or wrong, always came down to money; his money, as he often put it. She was tired of hearing those two words.

Holding back as much of her anger as she could, she addressed his money talk once and for all. "Your money? You think you made that money and achieved success by yourself because you were on the court?"

"Honey, that's not what I'm saying," Tellis said, trying to explain.

Moriah gladly cut him off with her hand.

"You had your say, now I'm having mine," she said with anguish. "What about me and the rest of your family who have supported you from day one? What about all of the times our kids longed for more time with you, but they sacrificed just as I did knowing how much your career and taking care of us meant to you. I love you for everything you've done, achieved and made of yourself, but I love you most for who you are - a man I fell in love with around the same age as our son is right now. You found love and he should be able to do the same on his own terms. We've raised him right and we have to respect who he decides to fall in love with and when and I hope that's the last time you open your mouth and proclaim your money to me," she said harshly.

When Tellis came closer to her as they stood arguing in the living room of their eight-million-dollar mansion, Moriah knew that she'd struck a nerve with him and he'd realize he'd gone too far.

"Whoa, I'm sorry. That was a poor choice of words and I

didn't mean it the way it sounded. I am because of you and how you held our lives in check all these years and I love and respect you for that." Tellis hoped his words were ringing true even though he could feel the tension in the room and no weapon, no matter how sharp, could cut through it right now. He needed to choose his words carefully. "When we fell in love, I had nothing and we achieved everything together. I would never, ever discount your role in the life we've built as husband and wife. I am, because we are. You have been my rock, my love, my support and my best friend since I was a teenager."

Moriah paced across the cream Persian rug in the center of the floor and tried her best to contain her anger at him.

"Then I don't understand why you can't see the same love between Ethan and Valencia."

Moriah stared as Tellis joined her in pacing around the room. They haven't had an argument like this in years and this latest quandary was one of his worst. Trying to rap her mind around the repercussions of his actions, she walked over to the fresh flowers she had been arranging when he walked in and told her what he'd done, interrupting her peaceful morning. The yellow and white arrangements strategically placed around the room brought out the gold, beige and cream color scheme of the room. For a split second, her anger had her thinking of picking up one of the crystal vases and tossing it at him to relieve the stress the conversation was causing. She would not give in to him on this and she would not placate him by making him think she was being the dutiful wife and following his lead. She stood her ground even when he walked over to her with his begging face and pleading eyes.

"Honey, she's not the one for him and you know it as much as I do, though you refuse to admit it because you want him to be happy. I do too, but that doesn't mean his happiness lies with the first pair of huge tits and big round behind that comes his way."

Moriah turned in slow-motion like characters do in a scary movie, tilted her head and looked at him sideways.

"So, you're looking at her body parts?" she asked.

Hearing that 'no joking' sound in her voice, Tellis took a step back. They have never been physical with each other, but he had a feeling his last foolish comment could cause her to slap him and reign back in his common sense. He was still putting his foot in his mouth. She was already angry for what he'd done and adding to that, what he'd just said, could cause a fight. He laughed it off to show her there was no need for her anger to boil over as he raised his hands in surrender.

"Don't go there – you know better and you know what I'm saying. The only thing Ethan sees is beauty, but he misses the fact that she has nothing else going for herself. Her family barely scrapes by. This girl lives in a tiny, rundown house with seven other people, a house I understand often has no electricity because they can barely pay their bills. You don't think she sees her ticket out of that through Ethan? Her mother works a just above minimum wage job and what I was able to find out about her father is that he doesn't even have a job. Even if they don't spot Ethan's potential, they know who he is and who we are and I assure you, that girl is being pushed to trap him by any means necessary. I won't have that for my son. He's taking a risk every time he lays up with that girl."

"You don't know that they're doing that."

This time Tellis looked at her sideways. "Trust me, I know and I also know that's a part of our son's life you don't want to hear about, but I'm on top of it. There will be no little Bennett's running around calling our teenage son daddy," he snorted.

Moriah didn't want to know about her son's escapades and moved beyond that discussion. She decided to let Tellis deal with their sons when it came to that.

"You've met her a handful of times and not once have you ever taken the time to get to know anything about her. You dismiss her and have never been shy about the fact that you don't want Ethan with her. I at least try to support his choice of a girlfriend by being cordial. Now, you're playing a dangerous game. I've always stayed back and let you deal with the boys while I focused on this modeling career that Esha wants to have. When you weren't on the road, I loved the time you spent with the boys, but now Ethan has the chance to make decisions regarding his own life and I've begged you to let him do it. You've pushed back on that and I've relented, now regretting my decision to do so. How could you play Russian roulette with our son's life?"

"I'm not playing anything. What I am doing is making sure that Ethan makes the right decisions when it comes to his life and career. Ever since he was a little boy, he has wanted nothing but the chance to play professional basketball. I've done everything to help him get there including being his personal coach through the years, getting him on the best local teams, encouraging his talent and letting him know that the world was his, and it is. This young girl can ruin everything for him and you're willing to sit back and let him ruin his future for a piece of..."

222

Moriah turned around so fast, she almost gave herself a whiplash.

"Don't you dare say that next word, not in this house. You know how I am about that kind of language directed at any woman, whether you respect their character or not," she said angrily.

Tellis caught himself and immediately apologized. He never disrespected a woman and even in anger, he knows he shouldn't and never in the face of the woman he loved.

"I'm sorry, baby. I was spouting in anger and I didn't mean anything by it. I would never, ever do that," he implored.

"I'm sorry to interrupt, but Mr. Bennett, you have a call, sir."

Moriah and Tellis looked over at Sarah, a woman who had been with them for years taking care of their household, as she entered the room. Tellis looked at her looking for any sign that she'd be angry if they continued the discussion later.

Moriah waved him off. She could use a break from their argument. "Go ahead and take it. It will give me a few minutes to tamper my anger down a few notches."

To calm her nerves after Tellis walked out, she walked over to the nearest chair and sat down, still fuming and wondering how they were going to get beyond this.

Enjoy this excerpt from "Heartthrob" – another romance novel from Cheryl Barton

"Mr. Weston, can I get a moment of your time?" a voice shouted.

"Cade! Over here please," another voice bellowed in the crowd.

"Cade, what was the most challenging aspect of your most recent film?" a male shouted over all the other voices.

"What do you like most about being Cade Weston? Is it being an actor, running your own record label, having a successful apparel line or the countless number of women who throw themselves at you daily?" a female voice shrieked.

"Can I have your baby?" yelled another.

Cade chuckled. That question he heard almost daily.

"Mr. Weston, what's next for you, is it a new movie or a brand-new business venture?" another voice hollered.

"Mr. Weston, are you single? I have a daughter and I think she'd be perfect for you!"

Cade smiled as questions were being thrown at him from the crowd that gathered outside of the Los Angeles television station. It was daytime, but he had just wrapped up the taping of his appearance on a late-night talk show. He was told to expect the crowd once word got out that he would be there. He expected a crowd, but nothing like what he encountered as he exited the building while his security team made a path to get him into the waiting limousine.

"Cade, what do you think of the nickname everyone has given you, calling you 'Heartthrob'? I hear it's because of the number of broken hearts you leave behind and the throbbing bodies women and some men experience just by getting a glimpse of you?" yet another voice shouted.

Cade stopped in his tracks at hearing himself being called 'Heartthrob'.

Recently, that pseudonym had been plastered on the cover of every magazine and news story written about him. He liked it, especially when people tried to define the title with their own characterization. He found it hilarious every time he read a new story about him and his sexual prowess, something that kept his name in the headlines.

"You don't have time to stop and answer questions, Cade," Abby, his personal assistant said, urging him to keep walking.

Cade knew she was right and though he was tempted to answer some of them, he continued on to the limousine and got in followed by Abby and Aaron, his chief of security.

"That is some crowd, especially this early in the morning," Aaron said.

Aaron was not only Cade's chief of security, but also one of his best friends since their college days.

"It is and I am who I am because of crowds like that."

"I see this heartthrob thing isn't going away. I'm beginning to believe you're really enjoying the title, brother," Aaron said slyly.

Cade didn't answer, but gave his friend a slick smile. Being labeled a heartthrob and plastered on the cover of magazines certainly had its benefits and he had the bank account and the sex life to prove it.

"I plead the fifth," Cade said with a smirk.

"What's on the agenda for today?" Aaron asked.

"I'm going home to work out and then I believe I have

several meetings at the record label. My artists are climbing the charts and because of that, we've been getting in demos from aspiring artists from around the world. There are a few my team, who has the responsibility for finding new talent, want me to hear. Then, later tonight, I'm going to be eye candy on the arm of Ms. Diamond at a fundraising event. Does that about cover it Abby?" he asked turning toward her and making sure he hadn't left anything out. He noticed she had yet to lift her head from her cell phone, no doubt booking him for another public appearance somewhere. He didn't question her; he just followed along with however she planned out his life.

"That's pretty much it. You asked me to clear your calendar after the event with Ms. Diamond tonight."

Aaron knew what that meant. Cade was often called on to accompany some of the most beautiful women in the world to events to keep the buzz about them in the media and it always worked. He knew that Cade believed that all press was good press in Hollywood. He had, after all, recently been name the sexiest man on the planet. Everyone wanted to be seen with him and all women wanted to get under him, literally. Aaron had a feeling Diamond would be engaging in both before the evening was over.

"Abby, can you get my usual suite ready for tonight and since I'll be entertaining, roll out the usual including my staple gift. Check to be sure it's not one that I've given Diamond in the past."

"Do you want me to add flowers this time as well?" she inquired.

Cade thought about it and knew it wouldn't be necessary with Diamond.

"No flowers tonight, but make sure my driver sticks around since she won't be staying the night."

Abby didn't respond or even react since they were all accustomed to Cade's penchant for entertaining and then moving on. This was going to be one of those nights. He would be doing his part to keep Diamond in the spotlight by being seen with her and in turn, she would spend the evening in whatever way he chose. He was Cade Weston, media mogul, box office smash, actor and of course, according to the everyone in the world who knows anything about him, a 'heartthrob' and he planned on living up to that name tonight. She loved working for the famous, Cade Weston and she loved that there was never a dull moment.

The Bachelor Series
Book 1 - Bachelor Not for Sale – Now available

Duron Knight agreed to take part in a bachelor auction held by his sister's sorority. Little did he know that he would find the woman of his dreams in the form of sexy bombshell Taija Charles, the woman in red.

Taija, in a room full of the sexiest men in Atlanta, has eyes for one handsome bachelor that no woman in her right mind could resist.

As sparks fly between them, can Duron put his unhappy past with women behind him and give his all to Taija? He may fight love, but Taija has plans to help him mend his broken heart with real love and a whole lot of lust.

Book 2 – A Designed Affair – Now available

In this follow-up to "Bachelor Not for Sale", Loren Knight has been engaging in a secret love affair with her brother Duron's best friend and business partner, Michael Bailey. He is everything she could want and more in a man, but she believes the risk is too great for any type of relationship with him beyond their steamy encounters behind closed doors.

Michael Bailey has been fighting his attraction to Loren for years. He has stayed away from her out of respect for his best friend and business partner. Now that he and Loren have finally given into the passion they have been craving, can Michael convince Loren that what they share is worth the risk of even Duron finding out?

Book 3 – A Perfect Combination – Now available

In this second follow-up to "Bachelor Not for Sale", Tyrone Davis is the king of one-night stands. The nickname, Mr. Love'em and Leave'em, given to him in his college days, still follows him as a top executive in the corporate world. He never believed in karma until it paid him a visit in the form of a very sexy and uninhibited one-night stand.

Victoria Alston couldn't forget the incredible night she spent with Tyrone Davis, someone connected to her best friends. In just one night, he stirred feelings in her she never thought she would ever experience. The next day, she disappeared, returning to reality and the fiancé she left back in Boston.

Tyrone and Victoria both soon discover that it wasn't just a one-night stand, but a perfect combination for the kind of love most people only dream about.

Book 4 – Love at Last – Now available

They had the perfect love...That's what Brian Knight thought of his relationship with Sherry Braxton until he looked up one day and she was gone and never wanted to see him again.

Two years later, he discovered that there is the possibility that Sherry may have been pregnant with his child. Hurt and angry at her deceit, he takes a flight to Baltimore to fight for his rights as a father and realizes that the love and passion they once shared had never died.

Is it possible he could still have the kind of love he thought would last a lifetime? Can he still have his love at last?

ABOUT THE AUTHOR

Cheryl Barton lives in Maryland and in her spare time she loves to read espionage novels, cook, watch Sci-fi movies, spend time with family and friends and enjoy Maryland steamed crabs.

Indulge in more romance and inspirational novels by visiting her website at www.cherylbarton.net.

Cheryl is a member of the Romance Writers of America – National Chapter and the Maryland Romance Writers.

Connect with the Author

Website www.CherylBarton.net or
www.crbarton.com
Twitter – @Author Cheryl Barton
Instagram – AuthorCherylBarton
Facebook at Author Cheryl Barton
Email – Cheryl@CherylBarton.net
Blog - https://mswriterinmd.wordpress.com/